pregnant at 17

Also by Christine Conradt

Missing at 17

Murdered at 17

CHRISTINE CONRADT

HarperTeen is an imprint of HarperCollins Publishers.

Pregnant at 17
 For information address HarperCollins Children's Books, a division of HarperCollins Publishers, 195 Broadway, New York, NY 10007.
www.epicreads.com

Library of Congress Control Number: 2017962818
ISBN 978-0-06-265166-2

Typography by Jenna Stempel-Lobell
18 19 20 21 22 PC/LSCH 10 9 8 7 6 5 4 3 2 1

First Edition

To David, for being the man I dreamt of finding my entire life. And for watching all the movies and making this the first book you've read since college. I hope it's at least half as interesting as whatever you read on ESPN. xoxo

pregnant at 17

ONE

BARS, BIKERS, AND BAD NEWS

"Can't go back. Still got an outstanding warrant there." Chelsea, trying not to eavesdrop, couldn't help but glance over at the leather-clad hulk of a man sitting a few bar stools away. At least 6'3" and sporting a dirty Hells Angels T-shirt, he sucked back a shot, the rim of the glass getting lost in his greasy goatee. He tilted his head to a scantily clad bleached-blond woman sitting next to him, and without lifting his drunken gaze from the breasts that were spilling haphazardly out of her bra, said, "We should just stay here in Philly."

Please don't, Chelsea thought as she turned to

scan the room, looking for anyone she knew. Chelsea Sheridans was slender and lanky with a creamy complexion—a wisp of a girl. Her long red hair was pulled back in a messy ponytail, and soft strands that had worked themselves loose framed her perfect face. At only seventeen years old, she knew she had no business sitting in a dive bar, but she'd been doing it since she was twelve, so it felt familiar. And because she could easily pass for twenty-one with her long legs and calm demeanor, no one ever questioned what she was doing there. Unfortunately, she didn't see a single person she felt like talking to. A few of the regulars, including a lady she liked named Dahlia, whose husband died from cancer the year before, were tucked down at the end of the bar and deeply involved in a conversation Chelsea couldn't hear. Dahlia was laughing and seemed happy, which was rare, so Chelsea decided not to interrupt.

Chelsea looked back at her phone. No new text messages, no calls. She looked at the background on her phone, a photo she'd taken of a single weed with a tiny white blossom that had grown up through a crack between the panels of cement in the sidewalk. She wasn't sure why, but seeing it made her feel hopeful and so she'd snapped a quick pic. She didn't feel quite so hopeful tonight, though. Seeing the same faces night after night made her feel stuck. With millions of places in the world, this is where these people chose to come. They didn't evolve or grow. They just got older. Even the weed changed more than they did. Chelsea didn't want to be like these people. She didn't want to get stuck like they were, eventually convincing herself that this was the best she could do. Every minute she spent there brought her closer to doing exactly that. *Oh god. Why am I even here?*

"You filthy cheater!" A voice boomed from the back as Chelsea blew out a sigh and slipped her phone back into her purse.

Several patrons, including Chelsea, swiveled around to see where the accusation was coming from. A short bald guy was pointing a finger at an older man wearing a bandanna on his head. They both held pool cues. Another argument emanating from billiards. *How unique*, Chelsea thought as she sighed and swung herself back around, ignoring them. Where some girls would freak out at seeing bar fights that started with words exchanged over beer-stained pool tables and drunks who suddenly pass out and drop from their chairs onto the dirty floor, none of it bothered Chelsea. She'd seen much worse. And not always at the Lucky Lady.

Chelsea inhaled the smell of stale cigarette smoke and blew out a sigh as she picked at the fuzzy little nubs on her faded maxi skirt. Rascal, the bartender, had been pouring drinks nonstop for the past half hour and without him to chat with, she was bored. She finished her vodka-cranberry and slid the empty glass back and forth between her hands, spinning it before letting it tap against her black-painted fingernails and chunky silver rings, hoping it would get his attention. It did.

"Try this." Rascal grinned as he set two shot glasses in front of her.

"What is it?" Chelsea asked, sniffing the booze. "Tequila? I hate tequila."

"You'll like it. It's smooth," he assured her with a wink.

Chelsea's eyes narrowed as she looked into his weathered face. When Rascal told her something was "smooth," it usually meant "overpoweringly strong." *Why not?* she thought. Maybe after a shot or two she'd cheer up a little. Chelsea lifted her glass and clinked the rim against his before knocking back the shot that was not, as she had predicted, in any way smooth. Coughing, she wiped her full pink lips with the back of her hand. "Good god, that was horrible," she choked. Rascal laughed.

As he picked up the glasses with hands covered in faded tattoos and moved down the bar to a waiting patron, Chelsea noticed a crusty, rough-looking man with wiry black hair slinking his way toward her. She immediately turned her head in the opposite direction, hoping he'd think she was busy doing something else and not try to talk to her. No such luck.

"Whatchya drinkin', sweetheart?" the man said with a tinge of a southern accent. Chelsea turned to him and was hit by a wall of stank breath—cheap beer and what was it? Sour-cream-and-onion potato chips? Rotting teeth? Nauseating.

Before she could answer, Rascal was right there. "Not interested," he said in a serious tone.

"Let her speak for herself. What? She don't got no tongue?" The intoxicated man wobbled precariously and grabbed the bar to steady himself. His glassy eyes darted back and forth between Chelsea and Rascal. Rascal leaned closer to the man and gave him a threatening look. Taking the hint, the guy made a sloppy hand motion suggesting Chelsea wasn't worth the hassle and then slid his way down the bar to chat up some less attractive, but more receptive, barflies.

"I can handle that stuff myself, y'know," Chelsea said, matter-of-fact.

"You know your dad expects me to look out for you," Rascal responded as he picked up her empty vodka glass and dropped it into a sink full of soapy water. The truth was, Chelsea appreciated that Rascal kept her safe like a big brother would, but she wasn't a child anymore. She'd basically been taking care of herself and in some ways, her father, since her mother died ten years ago.

Chelsea twisted around to get a view of her father, who was at the far end of the bar flirting with a woman wearing too much makeup and too little clothing. She watched as he pressed his large frame against the woman's back, leaning over her, helping her line up a shot on the pool table.

"I guess he's pretty busy right now," she spat, annoyed.

"He cares about you. Don't ever doubt that," Rascal stated with quiet confidence. Not in the mood to argue, Chelsea grabbed the patchwork purse off the back of her chair and made her way toward the pool table. She could feel the ogling eyes of several of the men bore into her as she walked past.

Stepping up to her father, Chelsea waited for him to acknowledge her.

"There you go. Just like that," he said to the woman bent over the table as she clumsily lined up a shot. *I've never seen anyone hold a pool cue like that*, Chelsea thought as the woman tried to balance the stick between two fingers. Chelsea watched as the woman took the shot, missed horribly, and then made a dramatically sad face.

"Poo," she said. "I'm terrible at this."

Yes, you are, Chelsea thought to herself. *You should pack it up right now and let me have a word with my dad.*

"You'll get better. Don't worry. I'm gonna teach you," her father assured the woman who, clearly not picking up on Chelsea's telepathy, didn't seem to be going anywhere.

"Dad," Chelsea said, folding her arms across her chest.

"Yeah, honey, what is it?"

"I'm going home. Can I have money for a cab?" Chelsea asked in a tone that let her father know she'd had her fill of the Lucky Lady for one night.

"Dom, it's your turn, man," a Latino man with

shoulder-length black hair said from across the billiards table, trying to hurry him up.

"The table's not goin' anywhere. I'm talking to my daughter," he responded. The man put his hands up in mock surrender and went about refilling his glass of beer. Chelsea's father turned back to her. "Is everything okay?"

"Yeah, I'm just . . . bored." That wasn't the entire truth. Yes, there was a certain ennui that came with sitting on a ratty bar stool night after night, but it was more than that. There was also the anxiety building in Chelsea because she hadn't received a single message from her boyfriend, Jeff, the entire night. Chelsea had tried all evening to push that out of her mind, but now she just wanted some time alone.

"Sure, sweetie, sure," her dad said as he extracted a crisp one-hundred-dollar bill from his wallet. "I'll be home later. Can you stop over at Mikey's and grab me a carton of cigarettes? I'm almost out."

Chelsea managed to flag down a taxi immediately and directed it to Mikey's, a run-down convenience store with a myriad of signs advertising specials on eggs, alcohol, and Pennsylvania lottery tickets. Chelsea handed the driver a twenty, accepted her change, and gave a two-dollar tip.

A tarnished bell above the door clanked unceremoniously, announcing her arrival. Mikey, who was sitting behind the counter, squinting over bifocals as he read a magazine, looked up and smiled as he saw Chelsea approach the counter. He grabbed his lacquered cane and with a shaky arm, slowly pulled himself up, and tugged his shirt down over his potbelly.

"Well, look at the beauty that just walked into my store. Lucky me!" Mikey said as a grandfatherly smile spread across his face.

"Hi, Mikey. How are you?"

"Any day that I'm here to see the sun go down is a good day," he said with exuberance. Chelsea loved his positivity. No matter how bad things were, Mikey always had a way of seeing the brighter side.

"I couldn't agree more," she said.

"Your dad out of smokes?" he asked as he tidied the counter, lining up a display of little palm-tree-shaped car air fresheners that hang from the rearview mirror. Chelsea nodded. "Got a few unopened cases in the back." Mikey started to hobble toward the back room with his cane when he suddenly stopped and swayed back to her, his bushy eyebrows turned down. "By the way, did you hear about Greg Foster?"

"No. What?" Chelsea could feel her heart rate pick up just at the mention of Greg's name.

"He made parole," Mikey said, his voice was laced with worry. "Gonna be out next week."

"That's three years early!" Chelsea spat, her mind clamoring to process the information. It couldn't be possible; Mikey must have his facts screwed up.

"Prisons are so overcrowded. I guess two years is enough for armed robbery these days." Mikey's words hung in the air like a dense fog.

"That's not right. Two years isn't enough," she murmured. She fought back a tear, feeling utterly helpless. Mikey smiled at her. It was the kind of smile that told Chelsea he was resigned, not happy.

"Well, he wouldn't have been put away at all if it hadn't been for you. I'm grateful to you. . . ."

"Hey, Chelsea." Chelsea and Mikey turned to see Mikey's grandson, Adam, step into the tungsten-lit room from the back hallway. The sparkle in Adam's aqua-colored eyes suggested he was pleasantly surprised to see her.

"Adam . . ." Chelsea said, the heaviness she'd just felt suddenly lifting a little. She'd practically grown up with Adam. When her father would bring her to Mikey's for a case of beer on sweltering Saturdays in the summer, she and Adam would chase each other around the storeroom until Mikey would coax them out with Popsicles. She'd always take the purple one and he'd take red, and they routinely pawned the orange ones off on her dad because he was the only person on the planet who liked orange-flavored Popsicles—at least that's what they believed at the time. They'd sit on a crumbling cement platform that Mikey referred to as the "loading dock," peel the sticky white wrappers from their Popsicles, and let their legs swing off the edge.

"I'll go grab those cigarettes," Mikey uttered with a grin.

"I can do it, Gramps," Adam responded, taking charge of the situation.

"No, no. You keep this beautiful young lady company," Mikey said, and shuffled away. Adam stepped a little closer to her.

"Long time, no see," he said, shoving his hands into the pockets of his baggy jeans. His lips curled up into a grin, revealing his perfect white teeth.

"Whose fault is that?" she teased. "I come in here at least once a week." He shrugged, letting her have that one. The smile never left his face.

"I'm taking the quarter off from school to do an internship. They're redoing the plumbing in the building, so I have a little time off. Thought I'd come back, hang out with Gramps." Had his voice become deeper since the last time she saw him? He seemed taller, or stronger, or just more mature. There was a confidence about Adam she hadn't noticed before. "I can't believe you're even standing here." As he said it, a lock of his thick black hair fell in front of his eye. He brushed it back and Chelsea noticed how the fabric of his shirt stretched across his biceps. Then he tucked his hand back into his pocket.

"Why's that?" she asked. Where else would she be? It's not like she ever went anywhere.

"Figured you'd be in Berlin by now. Isn't that what you wanted to do? Go see where your mom was born and all that?" She nodded, surprised he remembered that the last time they'd seen each other, she'd announced her plans to go to Germany, but that was almost a year ago and she wasn't any closer to saving for that trip today than she was back then.

"Düsseldorf," she corrected. "I'm gonna go really soon. I have it all mapped out." The "really soon" part was a lie, but the part about the map was true. Either way, Chelsea was embarrassed that she'd made no progress at all.

"Oh yeah? Well I have a trip planned for Europe next spring. Backpack through Austria and check out Amsterdam. You should think about coming along and we could maybe do a week in Germany afterward if—"

Before he could finish, Mikey emerged from the back with a carton of cigarettes. Adam abruptly stopped talking.

"Here you go, my dear," Mikey said as he handed it over, his hands trembling a little. They'd started doing that only a couple of months ago. The first time she'd seen it happen, she'd asked her father about it.

"It's not Parkinson's or anything, right?" It was the first thing that came up when she googled it and she prayed that wasn't the case.

"Might just be a side effect of medication or something. Don't worry about it. Whatever it is, there's nothing you can do to change it and if Mikey wants to explain it, he will." So Chelsea hadn't asked.

She fished the hundred her father gave her from her

pocket and handed it to him. Mikey opened the register to get her change. "Tell your dad to stop in when he gets a chance."

"I will. Thanks," she said. And then to Adam, "See you later." Adam surprised her by reaching out with a muscular arm and opening the door for her. The bell jingled again.

"Bye," Adam said. As she walked out of the store, she could feel Adam's gaze on her. Chelsea had always sensed an undercurrent of emotion between them. Maybe it was chemistry or maybe they'd just clicked as friends. Since neither of them ever mentioned it Chelsea had no idea where Adam stood. He'd never asked her out on a real date, and if he had, Chelsea had no idea how she would respond. How do you suddenly date someone that you used to throw water balloons at when you were nine years old?

It doesn't matter anyway, she reminded herself. Adam was definitely going to make some lucky girl very happy—if he wasn't already—but she already had a boyfriend. Jeff. The one who hadn't called or texted all day. She slipped her phone from her purse and confirmed what she already knew.

As Chelsea crossed the parking lot and walked

along the cracked sidewalk through the decaying neighborhood toward her house, thoughts of both Jeff and Adam disappeared. All she could think about was that in one week, Greg Foster would no longer be behind bars, no longer be locked up and away from society. He would be free; and that in and of itself was a very scary thought.

TWO
BAD THINGS HAPPEN TO GOOD PEOPLE

The walk from Mikey's store to the double-wide mobile home where Chelsea lived with her father wasn't long, but Chelsea knew it was best to stay alert and watch out for danger. A couple of months back, she'd been walking during the day when she spotted a stray dog scampering down the other side of the street. When she stopped, the dog stopped too and then let out a low, gravelly growl as it began to slink toward her. Lucky for Chelsea, a car came speeding around the corner at that moment and the dog took off running. Creepy dogs weren't the only kind of threat Chelsea looked out for on her walks home. It wasn't uncommon to see transients curled up on the porches of abandoned houses or hear the sound of domestic fighting through the open windows. Chelsea rarely felt unsafe, but that's because her father had taught her long ago to always be aware of what was going on around her.

Tonight, however, Chelsea was having a hard time paying attention to potential threats in the three-quarter-mile walk to the trailer park. She was distracted thinking about the night Greg Foster came running out of Mikey's store.

It had been so humid that night. Hot and still. Chelsea had gone to Mikey's on her way home from the Lucky Lady. She'd been about to cross the street when she'd accidentally dropped the money her father had given her for cigarettes and a carton of milk, and bent down to pick it up. That's when she'd heard a noise that cut through the quiet night air with a piercing ferocity. A gunshot. As Chelsea had bolted upright, she'd seen a lean man run out of Mikey's store with a plastic bag in his clenched, gloved fist. It had been hard to see clearly but she was sure he had a pistol in his other hand. She'd watched, breathless, as the man in a gray hoodie and black jeans peeled off his ski mask and looked around frantically. She'd recognized him instantly. There hadn't been a shred of doubt in her mind who it was. Greg. The brother of a girl—Lauren—she'd gone to school with since eighth grade. Greg was several years older than they were, but she'd seen him plenty of times around the neighborhood and at parties, and had even spoken to him once or twice. Until now, she'd never thought much of him other than that he came off a bit full of himself and she had no desire to spend much time with him. When she saw Greg's angular face come out from under that mask, Chelsea had gasped, the gunshot still ringing in her ears.

A moment later, a black car with polished rims and tinted windows had pulled up, Greg hopped in, and the driver sped off. Still reeling, Chelsea had watched it disappear around the corner, rooted to the ground until all she could hear was the fading roar of the engine, and finally that was gone too. Silence. Thick, heavy silence.

Oh my god! Mikey! Chelsea's instincts had kicked in at lightning speed. She'd raced across the street and burst into the store. At first the place looked empty. *Where is he? Please don't let him be dead!* Just the possibility of finding Mikey dead had stopped Chelsea in her tracks. Then she'd heard a groan. *A groan! He was alive!* She'd slid around the counter and stopped as the tips of her boots had met with a pool of blood. Mikey was lying on the floor, his hand weakly covering his hip where a dark, circular stain was growing. He'd looked up at her, desperate. His eye was red, his cheek cut open and bleeding.

"No!" she remembered screaming.

"He shot me," Mikey had struggled to speak, still covering the hole in his leg with his hands. Eyes stinging with tears, Chelsea'd forced herself to look away—to look for her phone. She'd felt for her pocket, it wasn't there. *Where was it?* She'd just had it a few moments ago. Spotting the worn handset for the cordless on the counter next to the empty cash register, she'd carefully stepped over Mikey, snatched it up, and punched out 911. *God, there's so much blood*, she'd thought. She'd needed to do something to slow the bleeding or he wouldn't last long enough for the paramedics to get there.

As Chelsea waited for the dispatcher to pick up, she'd looked back down at Mikey. The pool of blood beneath his lower body was growing. She'd run through the store, past a toppled candy display, and grabbed the first thing she'd seen that could help stop the bleeding—a kitchen towel. It had a turtle in a chef's hat printed on it, and when she'd pressed the towel over Mikey's pants and the hole in his hip underneath, the turtle turned crimson.

"Nine-one-one. What's your emergency?" *Finally.*

"Yes, I'm at Mikey's Market on Sixteenth Street. It just got robbed and the owner's been shot." The words had flowed out of Chelsea without hesitation. Even in the midst of crisis, Chelsea had a way of staying calm and cool.

"Is he breathing?"

"Yeah, it looks like he was just hit in the leg or the hip. I can't tell. But he's bleeding bad."

"I'm dispatching an ambulance. Did you see who robbed the store?" the dispatcher had asked. His voice was monotone, emotionless.

"Yes. I know him! His name's Greg Foster and he got into a black car with someone else driving. They turned right onto Bartels Avenue." Mikey'd moaned again, but Chelsea continued to press the towel against his leg. She'd looked down when she felt something sticky, and realized the blood had started to seep through her fingers.

"The ambulance is coming. You're gonna be okay."

Chelsea had tried to hide her fear that Mikey's life may end right there. She'd set the phone down and placed her right hand over her left, putting more pressure on the towel.

A loud honk jolted Chelsea from her reverie. Two obnoxious guys in a car laughed as they passed, thrilled that they could scare her into jumping.

"Nice ass, baby!" one of them yelled as the car sped off down the street. Rattled more by the memory of Mikey than the harassment, Chelsea suddenly felt alone again. Eager to hear a familiar voice, one that would assure her that everything would be okay, Chelsea pulled out her phone and composed a text to Jeff: *Hey. You around? Can you please call me?*

By the time Chelsea stuffed her house key into the lock on the front door, ten minutes later, Jeff had still not responded. She went inside. It wasn't much but it was familiar. She tossed her father's carton of cigarettes onto the little round table for two that separated the kitchen from the living room, and locked the front door. She considered bolting the chain as well, but decided not to. Hopefully, her father would be home soon from his night out, and she didn't want him to be locked out.

She thought getting inside would make her feel more at ease, but it didn't. She wondered how she'd ever feel safe again now that Greg would be free to go wherever he wanted. *Had he forgiven her for testifying against him? Would he come after her?*

Chelsea went from room to room turning on the lights. There were only four windows in the trailer: one in her room, her dad's room, the kitchen, and the living room. She checked to be sure they were all secured. They were, but seeing how flimsy the locks were only made her feel more anxious.

You have at least a week before you need to be scared, she told herself. A week. Tonight, Greg was behind bars. Tonight, she didn't have to worry.

Chelsea opened the fridge and pulled out a half-eaten tuna melt she'd made the day before. Popping it into the microwave, she watched it slowly rotate around. *Just like my relationship with Jeff*, she thought. *Around and around, going nowhere.* When the cheese began to bubble and drip down the sides, Chelsea pulled the plate from the microwave, and checked her phone once more, hoping that Jeff had responded.

Instead, her text went unanswered.

Chelsea took a bite of her sandwich as she sank

back on the battered gingham sofa and kicked off her shoes. Deep down, she knew why Jeff wasn't texting her back. He was probably with his wife. Whenever he didn't text back right away, that was the reason. Chelsea flipped on the TV, trying to distract herself from thinking about the man she loved sitting across from another woman. She pictured his strong jaw and thick build. He looked so sophisticated—like a man, not the pimply faced little boys who went to her old high school. He was confident and mature and, unlike her father, polished. She loved how he looked in a suit and tie, and how his fingernails were always perfectly clean.

The image of Jeff sitting across the table from his wife as they sipped wine and chatted about their workdays sent a pang of jealousy through her. She had never seen his wife, not even a photo of her, but Chelsea imagined she was stylish and beautiful. Not to mention educated and refined. The only thing Chelsea knew about her was that she was a veterinarian who worked long hours and made good money. *Maybe they aren't having a good time*, Chelsea hoped. According to Jeff, there were no laughter-filled dinners with his wife and there hadn't been for a long time. Jeff's wife had some big-time sports-agent boyfriend in Manhattan who Jeff pretended he didn't know about. The guy had a private plane and was always whisking her off to New York for long weekends when she wasn't busy working. Jeff had been lamenting about it just last week over dinner.

"It's disgusting," he'd said as he slid his fork into his risotto. "She talks to him on the phone right in front of me, acting like it's one of her girlfriends. I could do the same, you know. I could flaunt you in her face but I don't. Out of respect."

Chelsea'd studied him as he took another bite. "She still doesn't know about me?" She tried to keep the tone light, but she was pretty sure she hadn't. She couldn't help it. There was no way to ask without it sounding naggy, at least to Jeff.

"No. I told you. My lawyer said to keep it under wraps and act like everything's fine until it's time to drop the bomb and serve the papers."

Chelsea'd picked at her seafood linguine, wondering what she should say next. It had been at least a month since she'd asked the question and this was the same answer she received then: the lawyer's advice reigned supreme.

"I just, I don't know . . ." she had said, talking through her thoughts.

"You just what?"

"I just hate being your dirty little secret."

"You're not that," he'd assured her, and ran his fingers through his short brown hair. It was something he tended to do when he was frustrated. "Things are going to be much better for both of us if I maintain leverage in this divorce. There's a lot at stake and it's complicated. Assets, pensions, intellectual property. Unfortunately, I didn't have the foresight to get a prenup. If I had, this would already be over."

Chelsea'd nodded and sat back in the plush chair. She'd looked around at the other couples speaking softly to each other, gossiping, sharing desserts, sipping champagne as they celebrated whatever good thing had just happened in their lives. Jeff must've noticed because he'd looked around as well, seemingly curious about what had caught her attention.

"I don't want to talk about it anymore. I'm here with you and I want to focus on us. You have no idea how much I look forward to seeing you. You look beautiful tonight, by the way."

Chelsea'd smiled and looked down at the simple black dress she had on. She'd found it last year at the Goodwill store tucked behind some sundresses on the rack. It wasn't a designer brand, but it might as well have been. It was sleek and classy, and after shortening the spaghetti straps a little, it fit her perfectly, hugging her body in all the right places. It was the only decent dress she had and she'd worn it out with Jeff before. Each time she put it on, she did something a little different—either added a jacket or a scarf or some jewelry, hoping to disguise it. That night, she'd slipped one of her mother's old silk blouses over it. The green one that matched her eyes.

"I love you. And your patience means a lot to me. Someday soon, this will all be over and we can operate like a normal couple." Jeff'd squeezed her hand, making a point of rubbing his thumb over her slim ring finger. "There's something missing, but it won't be forever." Chelsea had known he meant a wedding ring, and hearing him say it made her feel good about them as a couple. It was so easy to let self-doubt creep in, and it helped when he reminded her of his intentions to be with her forever.

The show on television ended and Chelsea realized she'd been so busy thinking about Jeff, she didn't even know what she'd been watching. Her sandwich sat, half eaten, on the plate, now cold. She glanced at her phone.

After eleven. Still no response from Jeff. She needed something to occupy her mind and decided to iron her uniforms for work. It needed to be done anyway.

Chelsea set up the ironing board to waist-height and plugged in the iron. They were the same ones her mother had used, a wedding gift she and Chelsea's father had received from some family member. Chelsea couldn't remember who. Little things like that came up often and that's when she missed her mother the most. Chelsea would think of things she wished she could ask her. Silly things that might have seemed unimportant except that when her mother died, the answers died with her.

Pulling one of several pink shirts sporting the Stella Luna Gelato Shop logo from the flimsy plastic laundry basket, Chelsea stretched it across the board and set the heavy soleplate of the iron down right there in the middle. An image of her mother, a pretty woman with the same striking red hair as Chelsea, ironing at the same ironing board as she watched *The Bold and the Beautiful*, flooded Chelsea's mind.

Suddenly, the memory faded. Then everything faded. Chelsea stepped back as her vision turned black. Her knees buckled beneath her. The hot iron slipped from her hand and fell to the floor as her eyes rolled up and back. Chelsea grabbed for anything she could, clenching her pink shirt. In moments, Chelsea lost consciousness and crumpled to the floor.

THREE
GOOD THINGS COME IN SMALL PACKAGES

Chelsea opened her eyes and realized she was staring at the dingy white ceiling. The stout smell of singed linoleum hung heavy in the air.

Chelsea sat up and looked around. Why was she on the ground? What had happened? How long was she unconscious? "Dad?" she called out meekly. No answer.

The iron sat a few feet away. Its timer had shut it off, but not before it melted a four-inch gash into the floor.

I must've fainted, she concluded, not sure what else would cause her to forget how she'd gotten onto her back on the floor. Chelsea grabbed the still-warm iron and climbed to her feet. She spotted her phone: 11:29 p.m. No calls or texts. *I must've been out for, what, five, ten minutes?* She looked down at her elbows. Was she bruised? Had she gotten hurt? She rubbed her fingers over them but didn't feel any pain. Chelsea drew her knees up to her chest, trying to decide if she felt pain anywhere else. No. As far as she could tell, she was perfectly fine.

Using the chair to steady herself, Chelsea climbed to her feet. She plucked the iron up off the floor and ran her toe over the disfigured linoleum. *What happened?* She wondered if she'd been so upset about the news of Greg Foster's release that she passed out. *Don't think about any of this any more tonight*, she told herself. *Forget about Greg and Jeff and sweet old Mikey who has needed a cane ever since he was shot in the hip. Go to sleep. It will all be there in the morning.* Tossing her work shirt back into the basket, she unplugged the iron and went to bed.

The ring of Chelsea's cell phone cut through the silence, waking her from a restless sleep. Her heart skipped a beat as she reached across the nightstand and fumbled to pick it up. It was almost three a.m. Jeff was calling.

"Hey," she answered, trying to make her voice sound like she'd been awake.

"Sorry it took so long to call." Jeff's voice was deep and soothing. "How are you?"

"I'm okay, I guess. I got really light-headed earlier and fainted." She didn't want to come across as being overly dramatic, so she kept her tone casual.

There was a beat of silence on the other end of the line. "That could be something serious. I think you should take the day off from work tomorrow and go see a doctor." His tone was sensitive, caring, but also firm. Although Chelsea agreed with his advice, she knew that wasn't an option. Her father had been between jobs for the past two months and he'd let their health insurance lapse. He'd explained that he'd get it again when he could afford to pay the premium but it was important that she not go to the doctor. Otherwise, he'd be on the hook for the bill, which could be really expensive.

"Maybe. . . ." She said it to pacify him. "When can I see you? I miss you so much." What Chelsea really needed right then was to lose herself in Jeff's embrace and rest her head on his warm chest as he stroked her hair. She loved that feeling. In those moments, lying next to him in a comfy hotel bed, she felt safe. She could shut out the rest of the world and all the problems in it, and just be.

"I miss you too. How about I get us a room tomorrow night? At the Randall Garden Inn downtown? We'll order room service, cuddle up with a movie . . ."

Yes. Yes, yes, and yes.

"Sure. What time?" she asked, wishing he'd come pick her up at that very moment.

"I won't get there till after five but you can check in right after you get off work at three." Chelsea smiled, feeling somewhat relieved.

"Okay. That sounds good."

"I love you," he said softly.

"I love you too. See you tomorrow." Chelsea ended the call. More relaxed now, she snuggled back into bed and closed her eyes. Like she did so often when she was going to sleep, Chelsea imagined what it would be like if her mother were still alive. She pictured her happy and healthy, sitting in a café on Königsallee, a boulevard Chelsea had seen in her mother's pictures of Düsseldorf, loaded down with shopping bags from stores like Bulgari and Gucci, sampling rich chocolates. Perched on a park bench near the canal, Chelsea imagined sitting next to her, laughing with her mom and gushing about her upcoming wedding to Jeff. They would toss bread to the ducks that would gather around their feet. Her mother beamed and laughed and tried to throw her crusts of bread to the duck way in the back. It was a nice scene, calming, even if it only existed in her head. Focusing on shutting everything else out, Chelsea exhaled and tried for at least a few hours of peaceful dreams.

"I propose a toast to my brother and his early release!" Lauren yelled over the music that blared from the speakers mounted to the wall of the garage turned party room, teetering drunkenly on the Formica table that barely held her weight. Lauren was a small girl with a slight build, but what she lacked in size, she made up for in ferocity. Lauren raised her bottle of vodka and the dozen or so party guests who crammed into her garage did the same. Wrapping her hand around her frizzy blond hair, she knocked back a gulp of booze, then she lost her balance and would've fallen if Roy hadn't stepped up and put a hand on her waist. She looked down at him and smiled. Roy smiled back, showing off the gold on his capped tooth.

"Come down off there before you bust your ass,"

Roy said with a grin, and extended his hand for Lauren to take. Roy was nice-looking and even though he, like her brother, was five years older than Lauren, he didn't have any problem flirting with high school girls. Which suited Lauren just fine. She'd hooked up with guys Roy's age several times before. And she knew Roy was a decent guy. After Greg was carted off to prison, he stopped by often to help out Greg's baby mama, Amber, giving her things like cash or diapers or other items she needed from time to time. Amber lived with Lauren and her mother, and her mother was so grateful for Roy's help, she invited him to dinner at least once a week. Lauren liked that he was loyal to her brother and her family. That meant a lot.

Lauren turned toward him. Gripping her hips, he lifted her off the table and set her firmly on the floor. She teetered again and laughed.

"Good behavior," she slurred, raising her bottle again. Like her older brother, Greg, Lauren had brown eyes and a slightly turned-up nose. Unlike her brother, she had trouble holding her liquor.

"Greg and good behavior? Now there's two things you'll never hear in the same sentence again," Roy teased.

"Whatever. You miss him as much as I do." There was sincerity in her eyes, even though it was hard to tell under the layers of black makeup. She glanced around at the group of Greg's friends scattered about, getting high. *These are his supporters*, she thought proudly. *These are his true friends. The ones who stood by him when the going got tough.*

"You got that right," Roy said, and pulled her down onto the sofa next to him. They sat in silence for a moment, watching the others party in Greg's honor. "You know I still see that bitch sometimes. The one that turned him in. . . ."

"Chelsea?" Lauren asked, her voice tinged with hatred. "Doing what?" The mere sound of her name caused a swell of anger to rise in Lauren. Chelsea lived only a few miles away, but she had successfully managed to avoid seeing her.

"Usually walking or sitting at the bus stop. Doesn't she go to school with you?" Lauren felt Roy rest his hand on her thigh. She didn't mind. Far from a smooth move, but at least he was making his interest clear.

"That ho-bag dropped out a few months after his sentencing. You can thank me for that. Did what I could to make her life hell." Lauren's lips turned up into a grin as she thought back to how she got a few other girls to harass Chelsea every chance they could. They'd leave disturbing drawings in her locker of a stick figure they'd named "Dead Girl" who had bright orange hair. Sometimes Dead Girl would be hanging by her neck from a tree, other times she was tied to a stake consumed by giant flames. The drawings weren't the extent of it. They stole her purse once when she got up to get a book in the library and plastered her phone number all over the walls of the bus station bathroom until Chelsea was finally forced to change it.

"What'd you do?" Roy asked, curiously raising an eyebrow. Lauren could tell he was impressed by her loyalty to Greg, but he didn't need to know the specifics. Loose lips sink ships. She'd always abided by that rule and never revealed details. Letting others in on the details are what got people into trouble. It was no one else's business, and she didn't know why most people found it so difficult to keep the specifics to themselves.

"Enough to make her drop out," she responded, intentionally vague. "She deserved it. Screw her." If there was one thing Lauren was one hundred percent sure of, it was that all of her family's problems stemmed from Chelsea's lie. If she hadn't made up that story about Greg robbing the convenience store, Greg would still be around to help out their mother and raise his own daughter. Lilah, Greg's baby girl, was only a year and a half old. She needed her father. The whole family needed him. His absence was felt by every single person, every day.

"Don't you be getting in trouble too," Roy said flirtatiously as he pushed her hair back and delicately pinched the plug in her ear. "I don't think you could handle prison."

"What? I don't look tough to you?" she asked, not really caring about the answer, and downed another gulp of booze. Roy's hand moved from her ear to her thigh, pressing his fingertips down hard. She could feel the warmth of his hand through her jeans.

"I think you act a lot harder than you are," he murmured, and kissed her neck. His breath was hot and wet on her throat and as he moved toward her ear, her spine tingled. Lauren wasn't offended by his remark. She didn't need to prove to anyone how tough she was. If they wanted to believe she was passive and delicate, it was to her own advantage.

"Then I guess you don't know me that well, Roy," she whispered coyly, letting her gaze drift seductively to his lips. From the way his body opened up to her a little more, she could tell her look had turned him on.

"That's true, I don't," Roy whispered back, caressing her cheek with the back of his hand. "You should give me a chance to get to know a lot more about you, tough girl."

"I'll think about it." She meant it, but it wouldn't be tonight. Tonight, she was celebrating her brother's freedom.

Chelsea stared down into the toilet waiting for the next wave of nausea to hit her. It came a moment later. She gripped the side of the bowl and violently threw up. Again. This was the third time that morning that she'd had to sprint to the bathroom. Maybe eating day-old tuna melts was a bad idea. Chelsea sat back on her knees, waiting for round number four. When it didn't come, she spun some toilet paper off the roll and wiped her mouth. Squirting double the amount of toothpaste she normally used onto her toothbrush, she vigorously brushed her teeth. Just as she spit the minty foam into the sink, there was a knock on the bathroom door. Twisting open the door with her free hand, she looked into the face of her concerned father. "Too much to drink last night?" he asked. Chelsea wiped her mouth with her towel.

"I didn't drink that much. Maybe the tequila was bad or something."

"Don't let Rascal talk you into trying that stuff. It'll rot your guts." Her dad pointed a thick finger at her to punctuate his advice and moved off down the hall.

By the time Chelsea finished ironing her pink shirt, getting dressed for work, and packing her overnight bag, the smell of frying bacon had permeated every corner of the trailer. She made her way into the small kitchen where her father was busy cooking.

"Want some breakfast?" he asked as he expertly cracked an egg with one hand into the skillet.

"I can make it," Chelsea offered. She figured he was probably tired after getting home so late the night before.

"I got it, sweetie. I may not be able to cook much, but eggs I can handle." He threw a smile over his shoulder and turned back to the stove top. Chelsea grinned. Her father had spent three years as a line cook at a busy restaurant in downtown Philly. He could cook pretty much anything and it was always good. Chelsea lowered herself onto a chair. Her stomach still felt queasy.

Her father poured a cup of coffee and set it in front of her.

"Thanks."

"So I got some good news," her father said, clapping his hands together the way he always did when he was excited about a new opportunity. "Joey came into the bar last night after you left, and he's heading back up to Alaska. Said they're not crewed up yet and I could go with him." Any hope that her father's news was actually good faded instantly.

"On the crab boat?" she asked, trying to hide her worry.

"It's a lot of money," her father said, and slid a fried egg onto a plate. He set it down in front of her.

"How long?" Chelsea asked.

"A few weeks. Just till the season ends. Leave in a couple of hours." A couple of hours? Just like that? No discussion? That wasn't nearly enough time to talk him out of going.

"It's so dangerous. Don't you remember what Joey said? People die and stuff."

"Nah, not if you know what you're doing." He dismissed her concerns as he sat down across from her and sipped his coffee.

"Do you?" she blurted out. Chelsea already knew the answer. He didn't. He'd never been on a crab boat before, and while her dad was strong and physical, he was too old for this type of work. He could be too impulsive, too confident. He lived in the moment without ever really considering the consequences.

"I'm gonna be fine," her father said, and patted her hand affectionately. "What is it you always like to say? The universe brought it to my doorstep? If I wasn't supposed to take it, Joey wouldn't have mentioned it."

"I suppose. I didn't expect you to take on my optimistic point of view." She regretted telling him about the universe bringing opportunities if this was the way he interpreted her words.

Her dad chuckled and topped off his own mug with a little more coffee. Chelsea exhaled and took a bite of her bacon. Her father was right about one thing: they desperately needed the money. And once her father set his mind on something, it was almost impossible to make him change it. Since she wouldn't see him for almost a month, she figured she better tell him what she learned from Mikey.

"Greg Foster's getting out of prison. Mikey told me last night. Two years. That's all the time he's going to serve." Her father looked up. She expected him to be as stunned as she was but he appeared more resigned than anything.

"How's Mikey taking it?"

"You know how he is." Her father nodded. He'd been friends with Mikey since before Chelsea was born. He knew Mikey well.

"Like I always said, justice system ain't worth a damn. Rob a man, mess him up so bad he can hardly walk, and you get a slap on the wrist. I got friends who've been in there a helluva lot longer for doin' what? Stickin' needles in their own arms. Tell me which is worse." He shook his head, disgusted. Chelsea saw his expression turn dark.

"He'd be crazy to try anything with you. He's gotta know you got a dad that would mess him up real bad." He said it more to himself than her, and Chelsea knew he worried Greg might retaliate. It was certainly a possibility. "Bad enough he sicced that psychotic Lauren on you."

"Maybe you shouldn't go," Chelsea offered, hoping he'd change his mind about Alaska. "Just in case he does try something."

Her father said, "If I could make money some other

way, I'd never leave ya. I'll ask Rascal to keep an eye on things. And you, well, you know how to keep yourself safe. Always be paying attention. I doubt Foster would want to do anything that'd put him back in the pen. Break parole and he's back for a lot longer than two years."

Chelsea hoped her dad was right. Greg was a criminal but he wasn't crazy. It was in his best interest to leave her alone and move on with his new life as a father. Popping the remaining bite of bacon into her mouth, Chelsea stood.

"I gotta go," she said, and gave him a hug. "Be safe up there, okay? I've seen those shows where people get their hands caught in the fishing cables and stuff." Her dad planted a kiss on her forehead.

"I'll keep my hands away from any such cables. Promise." Chelsea grabbed her overnight bag and slung it over her shoulder. Most fathers would notice the bag and ask where she planned to spend the night, but not hers. Chelsea and her father had an unspoken agreement that she never asked him that question and he never asked her. Neither ever brought anyone home to sleep over at the house. The house, as small as it was, was a sanctuary of sorts. Just for them.

Chelsea said a little prayer to the universe to bring her dad back safely. She opened the door and threw him one last look. He was sliding her uneaten egg onto his own plate. She hoped it wouldn't be the last image she'd ever have of him.

An hour later, Chelsea stepped off the city bus and darted through traffic as she crossed the street. Stella Luna was a small but popular gelato shop on a street known for boutiques and bakeries. When she arrived she saw through the window her boss, Liz, hurry over to unlock the door and let her in.

"We're out of raspberry sorbetto," Liz said as she twisted the *Closed* sign to *Open*. "Won't have any more until next Thursday."

"Good time for all those raspberry fans to try something new." Chelsea grinned. Liz giggled. Chelsea liked Liz. She admired that Liz, after a messy divorce, had scraped together enough money to buy a franchise and become a business owner. Chelsea genuinely wanted to help her succeed.

During a lull between customers, Chelsea decided to get advice from Liz. She told her boss that she'd fainted the night before, burned the floor with an iron, and then woke up sick as a dog. Liz, seated at her desk in the cramped back office, twisted around in her chair to face Chelsea.

"Are you pregnant?" Liz asked gently. Pregnant? The thought hadn't even crossed Chelsea's mind. Sure, she and Jeff were intimate, but she was on birth control pills. Plus, she'd never heard of someone fainting because they were pregnant. Throwing up, yes, but there were a million reasons people throw up. "I think you should take a pregnancy test," Liz continued before Chelsea could respond.

"No. There's no way I could be pregnant." As soon as Chelsea said the words, she knew it was a lie. Of course there was a way. Chelsea didn't like how Liz looked at her. She knew Liz could see through Chelsea's bravado to the uncertainty that lurked underneath.

"If I go buy you a pregnancy test, will you take it?"

"I don't want you to waste your money." Pregnancy tests were expensive. She'd seen them in the store before and remembered being surprised at how much it costs for a plastic stick that you pee on.

"I'll be back in ten minutes," Liz said as she grabbed her purse and left.

Chelsea walked back to the front to mind the shop. As she waited for a customer to walk in, she pondered what she would feel if she learned she was actually pregnant. Would she be excited? Scared? Confused? For some reason, at the moment all she felt was numb.

Liz returned with a pregnancy test, concealed in a small brown paper bag, as Chelsea was scooping vanilla gelato into a cone for an elderly man and his grandson.

"I'll get this," Liz whispered, and handed her the bag.

"I can take it later," Chelsea whispered back, and smiled at the little boy. "And what kind would you like, sweetie?" The little boy pointed at the bubblegum flavor, but before Chelsea could reach for another cone, Liz had snatched up the scoop and was taking over.

"Go ahead," Liz encouraged her, knowing she was stalling. With no other choice, Chelsea sighed and reluctantly took the paper bag into the bathroom.

Tearing open the box, Chelsea pulled out the plastic wand and instructions. She discreetly tucked the box back into the paper bag, crumpled it up, and dropped it into the trash.

So I just pull off the cap and pee on it. Easy enough. She reread the directions once more to make sure she hadn't missed anything important and then set them on the edge of the porcelain sink.

It was quiet except for the faint buzz of overhead lights as Chelsea waited for the results. Anxious, she stared down at the wand in her palm, hoping to hurry it up. *Come on, come on.* The directions said it could take up to five minutes, but this felt like ten or fifteen. Chelsea checked her phone. Three minutes. Ugh.

Deciding she couldn't stand the wait, she opened the door and walked out to the counter where Liz was restocking little pink plastic spoons.

"Here," Chelsea said, and handed her the wand. "You look at it." Liz smiled nervously and, taking the wand in her hand, pushed her glasses up on her thin nose. Chelsea tried to read her reaction, but there wasn't one. Liz looked up.

"It's positive."

For a brief moment, Chelsea felt as if the air had been sucked out of the room. She didn't know if she couldn't breathe or just forgot to.

"I'm pregnant?" she whispered. Liz nodded. Chelsea could tell Liz was waiting to see if she was going to explode into a smile or burst into tears. *I'm a seventeen-year-old, pregnant with a married man's baby. I should probably start bawling now.* But the tears didn't come. Chelsea wasn't quite sure what she felt, but it certainly wasn't sadness. Happiness? Maybe. Fear? Definitely. Uncertainty? For sure. Was any of this even happening? Was it even real? It felt more like a dream.

"Are you okay?" Liz asked, and gently set the wand on the counter.

"I think so," Chelsea said, unsure if she even heard the question.

"Let's go back to my office."

In a daze Chelsea followed Liz to the back of the store and lowered herself into the metal folding chair Liz kept in her office.

"I'm pregnant." She didn't realize she'd said it out loud until she heard the words escape. Different scenarios flitted in and out of her mind more quickly than she could hang on to them. *There is a baby growing inside me. Jeff's baby, our baby! A real baby. Well, right now it's just a clump of cells but in nine months or so, I'm going to be holding a baby in my arms and it'll be mine.* The amazement she felt was quickly replaced by a fear she'd never experienced before. Not the kind of fear she felt when the dog almost attacked her or when she thought Mikey might die, or even the kind she felt when she thought about her father being thrown over the side of a crab boat into the icy Bering Sea. It was the kind of fear that seemed to burrow deep down into the center of her gut, fear that she was not responsible enough to be a mother.

"What are you thinking right now?" Liz asked.

"That . . . I need to tell Jeff. I'm gonna see him tonight and I'll, I'll tell him." How was she going to tell him?

"Is this someone you've been seeing for a while?" There was concern in Liz's voice.

"Three and a half months," Chelsea said, feeling confident. She hadn't really thought about how long they'd been together until this moment. Three and a half months was a good amount of time, wasn't it? It was the longest relationship she'd ever had. The only boy she'd gone out with before Jeff was a kid named Patrick at her high school, and that had only lasted two months before she caught him kissing some girl at a party he didn't think she was going to attend. Besides, her father usually dated women for a couple of weeks. She felt good about her three and a half months until she saw Liz deflate a little and could tell Liz didn't agree. Chelsea suddenly felt the need to persuade her that her relationship with Jeff was stronger than it sounded. "But he's got a good job and he's really solid. He wants kids, too. He and his wife tried to have one a while back he said, but she miscarried and he was super sad about it. This is going to be all right. He'll be happy."

"His wife?" Liz responded, stunned. Chelsea quickly covered.

"*Ex-wife.* I meant ex-wife."

"Chelsea, be honest. Is this guy married?" Liz asked quietly. There was compassion in her voice, but anger, too. Chelsea hesitated. Saying yes made her look like a home-wrecker, the dirty little secret she never wanted to be. And it made Jeff look bad, too, like a cheater who can't be trusted. How could she explain their complicated dynamic in a way Liz would understand? Liz was honest and smart and had her life together in every way. What could she possibly say to keep Liz from judging her as the messed-up teenager stupid enough to get knocked up by an older married man? Oh god. Can you say "daddy issues"?

"It's just a matter of paperwork," Chelsea assured her. "They both want a divorce." Liz leaned back and Chelsea could tell she was skeptical.

"How old is he?" Another bear trap of a question. Chelsea wasn't sure how old Jeff was, but he was probably in his thirties. Liz would definitely hate him if she revealed that.

"I love him. That's all that matters," Chelsea explained defensively. "Everyone always gets so hung up on age and money, and none of that matters. Love is the most important thing. When you fill your heart with love, everything else falls into place." She lifted up her pant leg and showed Liz the tattoo on her ankle.

"What does that mean?" Liz asked.

"*Liebe überwindet alles*," Chelsea said with near-perfect pronunciation. "It's German. My mother's favorite saying. Love conquers all."

"Oh, Chelsea, honey . . ." Liz's voice trailed off. Chelsea could see the disappointment in Liz's face and knew Liz found her naive.

The jingle of the front door opening ended the heavy moment. Liz stood.

"I'll take care of it." Liz blinked back a tear and walked out. *She wants to cry for me*, Chelsea thought, embarrassed. But Chelsea didn't feel like crying. As she sat there alone, staring at the corkboard above Liz's desk peppered with gelato orders and sales reports and phone messages, she started to feel happier, excited, even. She was going to have a baby. A tiny little baby. Maybe getting pregnant was exactly what she needed. No more not knowing what to do at night except hang out at the Lucky Lady. No more watching TV alone on weekends when her father was away. Having a baby meant having it with her all the time, and that changed everything. But it wasn't just about not being alone. She was going to be someone's mother. She was going to have a child who needed her in a way no one else had ever needed her before. *What could be more important than being a mother?* she wondered. The void she'd felt since her own mother passed proved it. *And that will be me. To that baby, I'll be more important than anyone else in the world.* And once Jeff finalized his divorce, they'd be a family. A sense of purpose came over Chelsea that she'd never had before.

Chelsea could understand Liz's concern. To Liz, she was too young to have a baby, too young to give up her life to be a mother. But what Liz didn't understand was that having a baby is what gave Chelsea's life purpose. What was she losing, really? She'd known ever since she dropped out of high school that she'd never have a career where she made a lot of money. She'd probably end up doing exactly what she was doing now—scooping gelato for minimum wage until Liz decided to teach her to be a manager. But it didn't matter. Jeff made more than enough to support her and their child.

Chelsea pictured herself standing in the living room, ironing Jeff's clothes as she watched her child roll himself up in a rug on the floor. She'd kneel down and pick him up and take him for a walk in his stroller. They'd go around the neighborhood and she'd point out things to him like flowers and birds. Other mothers would stop and tell her how cute her baby is and they'd chat about which diapers work best and how many hours of sleep they get. It would be perfect. But that was too much to explain to Liz, or to anyone, really, except Jeff. Jeff would get it. He loved her and he would understand why this baby, however unexpected it was, would be a good thing for both of them.

This will all be okay, she told herself. *Jeff's gonna be happy when I tell him tonight. He really will.*

FOUR
DADDY ISSUES

Chelsea stepped into the Randall Garden Inn. She looked around, letting her eyes adjust from the bright afternoon sun to the softly lit lobby. There was an elderly couple standing at the registration desk, checking in, and a woman with a ball cap and yoga pants sitting in one of the oversize chairs, reading a magazine. Other than that, the place was pretty much empty. It wasn't overly shi-shi, but nice enough with marble floors and stylish furniture that Chelsea suddenly felt a little out of place in her gelato-stained Stella Luna T-shirt. She adjusted the strap of the overnight bag to cover the logo and made her way to the reception desk.

"May I help you?" the stout man behind the desk said with a smile.

"Hi. Yes. My boyfriend made a reservation for tonight."

"What's the name?"

"Jeff Clefton. It might also be under mine. Chelsea Sheridans?" The clerk pulled down the cuffs on his blue blazer and clicked away on his keyboard.

"Sheridans? With an 's' at the end?"

"That's right. An 's' at both ends." She was used to people misspelling her surname. At least Chelsea was pretty simple. After a few more keystrokes, he smiled.

"Yes, miss. I have your reservation right here. King-size bed, nonsmoking, room two fourteen. Second floor, turn right as you exit the elevator." Chelsea nodded as he slid a key across the counter to her. She liked staying at hotels. Everything about them felt luxurious. And she liked the way the front desk people treated her. Something about the way they talked to her made her feel special.

"Thank you," Chelsea said, and walked to the elevator, excited to start her evening and share her news with Jeff.

With a click, the door opened and Chelsea stepped into her new home for the next twelve hours. She was impressed. Against the wall was a king-size bed, a cloud of white pillows with scalloped edges perfectly arranged at the head. Chelsea dropped her bag onto the puffy white duvet that covered the bed and flopped down. It was as comfortable as it looked. Rolling over, she spotted the remote on the little bedside table next to the leather-bound room service menu and turned on the TV, hoping to calm her nerves. *How will I tell him?* she wondered. Chelsea wasn't sure if she should come right out and say it or wait until he ordered her a glass of wine and then explain why she wasn't drinking. She pictured Jeff's face when she told him that the thing he had wanted for so long was about to come true; he would be a father. He would smile and his eyes would light up and maybe he'd even get a tear in his eye.

"Are you serious?" he'd ask with the broadest smile she'd ever seen. And when she nodded, he'd place a hand on her stomach and they'd try to feel the baby together.

Chelsea adjusted the pillows behind her head and sank back. Would they have a boy or a girl? She'd been picturing the baby as a boy, but wasn't sure why. Was that mother's intuition? Did she inherently know she was having a son? What did Jeff want? What if it was twins? A boy and a girl? Two for the price of one! She smiled at the thought of balancing a chubby-faced little toddler on each hip.

Checking the time, Chelsea saw that she had another hour until Jeff arrived and decided she might as well take a bath. She ran her fingers over the terry-cloth bathrobe that hung behind the door in the bathroom before turning on the water in the Jacuzzi tub. As steam began to rise and fill the room, she caught a glimpse of herself in the mirror. Was she showing yet? Turning to the side, she studied herself. Her belly was as flat as a board. Peeling off her pink shirt, she looked again. Flat, flat, flat. And pale white. Chelsea pushed her belly out, wanting to see what she'd look like in a few months. But she didn't look pregnant. She looked like a skinny girl uncomfortably overarching her back.

Even as a child, she'd always been a skinny kid. She remembered when she was seven she had perused through some old photos with her mother right before she got sick.

"Look at me here," Chelsea had said, pointing to a photo of herself, holding a giant ice-cream cone and grinning at the camera. Her legs looked like two round hamburger buns glued to sticks.

"That was two years ago on the first day of school. My word. Look at those knobby knees. You were always falling down and scraping them up." Her mother had grinned. "For three years I carried Band-Aids in my purse." Chelsea'd laughed.

"I still have knobby knees."

"You weren't the most graceful or coordinated child on the playground," her mother had said, and winked. "But you were definitely the cutest and smartest. *Mein perfektes kind.*"

Chelsea smiled at the memory. Her mother always told her she was perfect. More than once she had told Chelsea, "Your flaws are as much a part of you as your attributes. There's no good or bad in any of it. It just is what it is."

Chelsea felt a familiar pang of longing for her mother. *I wish I could tell her about the baby. I wish she could be there with me at the hospital.* She'd walk around with the baby in her arms bragging about her grandchild. Life with a kid would be easier if her mother were still alive. A lot of things would be easier. Chelsea felt the hot sting of tears fill her eyes and she pushed the thought of her mom out of her mind.

Chelsea slipped out of her clothes and settled into the soothing bathwater. She wanted to relax and think of nothing.

Plucking the tiny plastic bottle of hotel-brand shampoo from the side of the tub, she twisted off the cap and inhaled its fresh, floral scent. It smelled so much better than the cheap shampoo she bought for her and her father.

After washing her hair, she lay back in the tub and pushed the button to turn on the jets. The warm water swirled around her. Closing her eyes, she thought more about what motherhood would be like. She imagined being at the park on a sunny day throwing a party for her baby's first birthday. There was a piñata and balloons and a cake in the shape of the number "1" and lots of people she didn't know yet but soon would—other moms—were bringing her child gifts wrapped in colorful paper. Her fantasy was abruptly interrupted with a thought. If she's pregnant now, what month will the baby be born? She counted eight months on her fingers and decided it would be May, maybe June. It would be a summer birthday, so a party in the park would probably be fine.

The more images Chelsea conjured up of her and

her child, the more she realized that everything was going to be okay. That was another thing her mother had taught her.

"Things happen the way they are supposed to," her mother would say when Chelsea showed any sign of impatience. "It's up to the universe. And the universe will always provide the right thing at the right time. *Das universum ist liebe, und liebe überwindet alles.*" Chelsea felt more at ease with telling Jeff when she reminded herself that the universe had wanted this. As soon as Jeff arrived, she'd throw her arms around him and deliver the good news.

With the bathrobe hanging off her thin shoulders, Chelsea slowly brushed out her long hair in the steamy mirror. That's when she heard the door to the hotel room open. That familiar hot, nervous feeling rushed up inside her again and she suddenly felt anxious. When he peeked his head around the corner and smiled that perfect, sexy smile of his, she lost her nerve. *Besides*, she told herself, *it doesn't make sense to spring this on him the minute he walked through the door.*

"I'm so happy to see you," he said and placed a long, passionate kiss on her lips. Trying to mask her anxiety, she squeezed his hand.

"I'm happy to see you, too." She felt his warm hands slip into her bathrobe and caress the sides of her waist. She kissed him again and let the robe fall to the floor. Picking her up, he carried her into the bedroom and laid her down on the bed where she and Jeff proceeded to make love.

When they were done, Jeff wrapped his arm around Chelsea and pulled her close. She snuggled even closer, pressing her cheek against his strong chest. She knew she had to tell him. He deserved to know, and every minute she went on acting like this was just another clandestine weekend together made her feel more and more guilty.

What should I say? she wondered. She was excited about the baby now but it had taken hours for her to peel away all the other cluttered-up thoughts and feelings to get there. She had to remember he was still married, and Jeff hadn't been shy about telling her he needed to take his time and do this divorce thing right. It was a lot harder than she thought to find the right words.

"I know you don't like to talk about it, but how long will it take before your divorce is final?" She turned and looked up at him.

"I know that's what you want and like I keep saying, that time is coming. But I need time to work out the details."

"More than nine months?" she asked, forcing the words out. She waited for a reaction, hoping for the smile she'd fantasized about. But Jeff stared at her with a stunned look. He abruptly sat up, putting distance between them as he faced her.

"What are you saying? Are you pregnant!?" Jeff's eyes darted back and forth as he spoke, searching hers. All of Chelsea's vibrant, blissful fantasies drained away. She nodded, scared to hear what he would say next. She hoped the words weren't too mean. She'd never felt more vulnerable than she did now and knew his words, if he wanted them to, could crush her. But Jeff didn't speak. Instead, Jeff bolted out of bed. He stood there, naked, rooted into the ground, unable to make eye contact with her.

"I know we didn't plan it but you said you always wanted a baby . . . that you were devastated when your wife had that miscarriage. . . ." Chelsea uttered the words slowly, hoping to convince him that the pregnancy could be the very thing he'd been waiting for.

"You said you started taking birth control pills.

Were you? What happened?" Jeff's tone was accusatory.

"Of course I took the pills—" she started to explain, shocked that Jeff was reacting like this.

"Every day?" he interrupted, making her feel even more defensive. No. She hadn't taken them every single day. There were a couple of days that she had hurried off to work and forgotten to bring them with her. After that, she decided to start taking them at night before she went to bed, but there was one night after getting back from the Lucky Lady that she fell asleep in front of the television and remembered to take it the next morning.

"Usually. I may have forgotten a few times. I mean, I'm human. . . ." Chelsea uttered, unsure what else to say.

"Chelsea! If I'd known that, I would've used protection myself! I trusted you." His voice was getting louder. The words dug deep, hurting her.

"Are you saying you can't trust me?" Panic began to rise up inside her. How did this moment, which should have been such a joyous one, turn into something so ugly? She watched as Jeff raised his hands as if trying to remain calm.

"I'm sorry. This is just really . . . unexpected." As

he spoke, he grabbed his pants off the chair and started to get dressed.

"Why are you so upset? I thought you'd be happy! You keep saying you want to marry me someday and we can have a family." The words were flowing now. She knew what she wanted to say. "I know it's sooner than we expected but it's still what we both want." Chelsea pulled her robe tightly closed as she watched him reach for his shirt. He stopped.

"This isn't at all what I want. I'm still married, for crying out loud!" Chelsea could feel tears welling in her eyes. She couldn't wrap her head around what he was saying. After everything he had said before about wanting children, it didn't seem possible that he would be so against the idea now. She scrambled to come up with an argument to convince him that he wanted their baby.

"You're divorcing your wife anyway. She has that boyfriend in New York. She won't care!" Chelsea blinked back the tear that threatened to spill down her cheek. Jeff just stared at her and she could tell there was something he wasn't saying.

"She doesn't have a . . ." His voice trailed off. "She won't understand." He was calm now, steady. Chelsea sat down on the bed. This was so far from what she had hoped for. What would her baby think, knowing that his parents were arguing over whether they wanted him? *I guess I deserve this*, she thought. *This is what happens when you get pregnant by a guy who is married to someone else.* That tear she was trying to hold back broke loose. She quickly wiped it away with her thumb. "How far along are you?" he asked, his voice softer.

"I don't know. Liz said I need to go to a doctor."

"Liz, your boss?" he asked, the tension returning to his voice. Chelsea nodded, unsure why she felt all over again like she'd done something wrong. "Who else have you told?!" The question surprised her. Was she supposed to keep it a secret? Pretend she wasn't pregnant?

"No one. But I feel like I should tell my dad. . . ." Chelsea hadn't really thought about what her father would say until this very moment. Would he be happy and angry? She'd been too consumed with sharing the news with Jeff to wonder.

"Your dad?" Jeff asked, his tone switching. "Why even involve him? This is about us." *Good. Finally. He realizes that.* It didn't change the fact that at some point she would need to tell her father, and before that, she'd most likely need to see a doctor. Even if Jeff would pay for the doctor visit, she needed her guardian to sign the paperwork.

"I'm pretty sure the doctor's office won't let me sign papers and stuff until I'm eighteen." She wasn't "pretty sure," she knew they wouldn't. She'd tried once while her dad was out of town working and she'd sprained her ankle. When she arrived at the office, they turned her away.

"Did you just say you're not eighteen?" Jeff asked. Again, she felt she'd done something wrong.

"I'm seventeen," Chelsea said.

"No, no. That's not possible. I met you in a bar! You were drinking!" Jeff took a few steps back, putting even more space between them.

"I've been doing that since I was fifteen," she said truthfully. She'd been going to the Lucky Lady with her dad since she was twelve, but she was fifteen the first time Rascal let her have a beer. At least she thought she was. It was hard to remember.

"Oh my god. Why the hell didn't you tell me?!" Jeff yelled, furious.

"You never asked! It wasn't like I was trying to keep it from you! And one time when we were talking about my mom being older than my dad, you said age didn't matter!" Why was everyone so hung up on age? She thought he was beyond that.

"It matters if you're *under*age! Jesus!" Jeff threw his hands up as if it were the most obvious thing in the world and she was an idiot for not understanding. "I'm sorry. I need time to think. I have to go someplace and just . . . think." He practically jumped into his socks, he was so eager to leave. Chelsea felt her panic rise a notch. He wasn't really going to leave her there alone, was he?

"You're leaving?" He didn't say anything. Just reached for his shirt and slipped it on. "No, please don't." She didn't want to be alone right now and she didn't want the man she loved to be this upset with her. Even though she had never lied to him, not once, she still felt like she had done something wrong.

"I'm going to call you tomorrow, okay?" Jeff said as he finished getting dressed. "Until then, do not tell anyone about me or the pregnancy. Can you promise?"

Chelsea couldn't absorb what Jeff was saying. All she knew was that she needed to find the words to make him stay. "Don't leave. I love you," she pleaded. As she got up to hug him, he held his arm out keeping her at bay. She'd never felt more desperate in her life.

"I really need some time alone right now. Okay? Please. Everything's going to be okay. We'll talk tomorrow."

"No. Jeff. Please!"

"We'll figure all of this out, all right? We'll figure it out. Just gimme a day or two." A day or two? He'd just said he'd call her tomorrow. Oh god, oh god. This was it. She knew she couldn't go two whole days without talking to him, without knowing what he was thinking. Why couldn't he just be as excited for the baby as she was? They'd created something beautiful together. Couldn't he see that? Couldn't he see that nothing else mattered? "The room's paid for. You can stay until checkout."

"Jeff, come on! I don't want to be here by myself."

"I gotta go," he said. With those final words, Jeff grabbed his bag and walked out. Chelsea watched the door shut. *Please come back. Just realize you've made a mistake and turn around and come back.* She waited for the doorknob to turn but it didn't. She could hear the faint ding of the elevator down the hall.

As she stood in the center of the room, surrounded by luxury, she'd never felt so alone. She was hurt and ashamed and terrified. And pregnant. What should've been the happiest day of her life had spiraled into something she didn't even fully comprehend. Chelsea fell down on the bed and sobbed.

A few minutes later when her cell phone rang in her purse, Chelsea scrambled to pick it up, sure that Jeff had changed his mind and wanted to talk things through. But it wasn't Jeff calling. It was Mikey's store. Afraid that it was more bad news about Greg Foster, Chelsea answered quickly.

"Hello?" She sniffed, trying to sound like she hadn't been crying.

"Chelsea?" Chelsea had been expecting to hear Mikey's voice, but it was Adam. "What's wrong? Are you okay?"

"I'm fine," she lied. "What's up?" She knew her attempt to sound chipper had failed miserably.

"You're seriously not fine. I can tell. What happened?" Adam pressed, his voice tender. She wanted so badly to talk to someone, but how could she tell Adam about the situation she'd gotten herself into? What would he think of her? She wasn't sure he'd understand, but right now, it didn't really matter. He was the one on the phone and willing to listen. Before she could answer, Adam piped in again. "I'm coming over to your house right now. I'll be there in fifteen." He sounded so confident and in control, ready to take charge. She needed that right now.

"No," she said quickly. "I'm not at home."

"Where are you?"

"I'm . . . I'm at a hotel. I just got into a fight with my boyfriend and he left. But I don't want to be here. Could you, I don't know . . . come get me and take me home?" At least at home she'd be able to cuddle up in her own bed, surrounded by her own things, and try to forget this night ever happened.

"Text me the address. I'm on my way."

FIVE
BYGONES NEVER GONE

"I can't believe he'd just up and walk out," Adam said, slinging Chelsea's overnight bag on his muscular shoulder. As they made their way through the hotel lobby, Adam quickened his step so he could reach the door before she did. As he opened it for her, she could feel the warmth of his protective hand on the small of her back. It felt good, gentle but strong.

She remembered the relief she had felt when she'd heard him knock on the hotel room door. She had no idea how he'd gotten there so quickly. He must've sped the entire way.

"Hey," he'd said cautiously when she opened the door for him. He took one look at her face and immediately pulled her into his chest, wrapping his arms around her and resting his chin on the top of her head. Her face had pressed lightly against his neck and she could smell the scent of his cologne. "Are you okay?"

"Yeah," she'd whispered, and felt his fingers lightly stroking her hair. She'd wanted nothing more in that moment than to melt into him.

"What the hell happened?"

"Come in and I'll tell you," she'd urged. He'd followed her inside.

"Are you kidding me?" he'd said, once she finished telling him the whole story. She'd told him about Jeff and how they met and what he'd done after she told him she was pregnant.

"Who leaves his pregnant girlfriend in a hotel room by herself?" Adam had asked, his bright blue eyes boring into her.

"I guess Jeff does." It had been all she could think of to say. Adam had shook his head, angry. Chelsea'd wondered if she was being fair to Jeff. Part of her felt the need to defend him so he didn't come across as a complete asshole. After all, she had sprung this on him.

And it was her fault for not taking the pills the way she was supposed to, right? "I think he just needed time. It's a lot to deal with."

"It's a lot to leave the girl to deal with by herself," Adam had quipped, clearly not buying into the justification. He'd stretched back in the chair and looked toward the window. She couldn't tell what he'd been thinking but she was sure it hadn't been anything complimentary about Jeff. Her eyes had lowered to his waist where the bottom of his T-shirt had lifted up, exposing his toned stomach. For a brief moment, she'd forgotten all about Jeff and wanted to slide her hands up under Adam's shirt and feel his chest. *What the hell am I doing?* The intimate thoughts about Adam had caught her completely off guard. She had a boyfriend who she loved. And she was carrying his kid. Yet the guy who had come rushing to help her when she felt alone was the boy she'd always thought of as family. It all felt twisted and messed up.

It wasn't the first time she'd had passionate thoughts about Adam. It had happened a few other times but she always brushed those thoughts aside, reminding herself that they were just friends—buddies who had known each other forever. Adam wasn't interested in her like that. Why would he be? He'd seen her with bad haircuts and sunburns and snot running out of her nose when she was sick and her dad had dropped her off at Mikey's house so he could go to work. She was sure there were much prettier, older, more sophisticated girls at Adam's college. Girls that were going to do more than scoop gelato for a living.

The first time she'd ever felt a tinge of jealousy over Adam was two summers ago when they were hanging out at Mikey's store and a pretty blond girl in a crop top had ambled in to buy a soda. As the girl stood at the soda machine with her long, perfectly shaped legs, she'd tossed her hair to the side and thrown a flirtatious look to Adam, who was stocking shelves. Adam didn't notice, but Chelsea had and it'd irritated her to no end. *Get your own*, Chelsea had thought. *He's mine.*

The second time was on the Fourth of July the year after that. Chelsea's father had brought a bunch of illegal fireworks from Missouri where he'd been working construction for a few weeks. Mikey had invited them to set them off in the parking lot in front of his store.

As Chelsea rummaged through the box, looking through the mass of M-80s and giant flowering cones, Adam had sidled up next to her.

"These are cool," he had said, and flashed a smile. As he reached into the box and pushed aside a few Roman candles, his hand had inadvertently touched hers and she felt a rush of excitement.

"Have you ever lived in China?" he'd asked.

"No," Chelsea'd responded, confused. "Why?"

"This one's named after you," he'd said, holding up a firecracker. She'd tried to see the writing on the front of the cardboard cylinder but he stood up and walked away with it.

It wasn't until her father had it positioned in the middle of the parking lot that she'd realized what Adam was talking about.

"Okay!" her father had shouted, a glowing punk in his hand. "This next one is called the Dazzling Damsel." As her father had knelt down to light the wick of that same hexagonal firecracker, Chelsea had glanced over at Adam, who was seated on Mikey's car. He'd smiled at her. She remembered quickly looking away. It wasn't until the firework was emitting a shower of red and gold sparks that Chelsea had mustered the nerve to look at Adam again. Through the falling embers, she could see him. He was leaning back, his hands pressed on the hood behind him, his perfect face tilted up. She'd wanted to go sit next to him but didn't have the nerve.

Not that any of that matters now, Chelsea thought as she and Adam crossed the hotel parking lot to his old red Toyota Corolla. The car was far past its prime.

"A real man would've been supportive. He should have sat with you and held you and talked through it." Adam opened the passenger door for her.

Chelsea paused, conflicted. On one hand, Adam was saying the very things she needed to hear and she no longer felt completely abandoned. On the other hand, Jeff was the father of her child. She didn't want Adam, or anyone else, to think he was a colossal jerk. And if he truly was, she honestly didn't want to acknowledge it either. Adam shut her door. She watched in the side mirror as he opened the trunk and put her overnight bag inside. Then he came around to the driver's door and slid in behind the wheel.

"What are you doing with a married guy, anyway?" he asked. His tone was more curious than accusatory.

"I don't know," she said, and waited for Adam to twist the key in the ignition. The engine made a strange, guttural noise when it started up, but at least it was reliable enough to get Chelsea back home. "He was in a bad marriage, his wife was cheating on him, and . . . I thought he sort of needed me." Although her answer wasn't particularly profound, it was the truth. One of the things that had drawn her to Jeff was the fact that she thought she could make him happy in a way his wife couldn't. Adam turned and faced her.

"Are you *in love* with him?" he asked, his eyes searching hers. Chelsea quickly averted her gaze and began fidgeting with the ring on her middle finger as she thought about the answer.

"I think so. I mean, he's everything I want. . . ."

"What *do* you want?" he asked. Chelsea thought for a moment about why she'd been so drawn to Jeff.

"Someone with a steady job, like the kind you wear a suit to and get up and go to every day," she said, thinking about her father's muddled work history. "Something that's not dangerous." She saw Adam raise an eyebrow and knew he was confused. He had no idea her father was off fishing the icy waters of Alaska. "Someone who likes to just sit in the grass and watch the sun set," she continued. "I'm sick of hanging out in smoky bars. I want someone who enjoys nice things, picnics outside, going places, that kind of stuff."

"How about someone who would be stoked if you told him you were having a baby? Someone who doesn't leave you hanging so he can go home to his wife?" Adam asked as he craned his head around to look out the back window as he pulled out of his parking space. His words were blunt and it hit home a little too hard. Chelsea started to tear up. He was right. She wanted that, but she didn't have it, and that made her feel bad, not just for herself but her baby, too. "I'm sorry. I shouldn't have said that," Adam apologized. "Look, I hope it works out with you guys. I really do."

"Thanks," Chelsea said softly.

"Just know that you deserve someone who will give you everything you want." *That's exactly what Adam would do for the girl he loved*, Chelsea thought. *He'd give her everything she wanted.* She didn't know why that thought, and the realization that she would never get to be that girl, made her feel so sad.

They rode the rest of the drive home in silence. Chelsea replayed Adam's statement in her mind over and over. *You deserve someone who will give you everything you want.* Chelsea was sure that Jeff was that guy. That once he had taken a moment to let the news sink in he would be excited about having a child. After all, he had said that he loved her. He had said that he wanted a child more than anything. But as much as she tried to convince herself that this would all work out for the best, she kept coming back to that simple phrase. *You deserve someone who will give you everything you want.* Did she? Did she deserve that? It seemed too good to be true.

As Adam's car slowed to a stop in front of Chelsea's trailer, Chelsea unclicked her seat belt.

"Thank you," she said. "For bringing me home."

Adam nodded but didn't say anything else. He seemed sad. Chelsea didn't know what to say either, so she opened her door and got out. Adam came around the car and opened the trunk.

"I got it," Chelsea said as they both reached for the overnight bag.

"I'll do it," he said firmly.

"Would you like to come in?" she asked as Adam walked her to her front door, hoping he'd say yes. Being with him made her feel better.

"I don't think that's a good idea." His voice was laced with regret. She understood. He had to be disappointed in her for getting herself into this situation, and he'd already gone out of his way to help her.

"Okay." Chelsea held back the tears that threatened to come spilling out. She watched as Adam slowly turned and walked to his car. She wanted him to look back at her, but afraid he wouldn't, she slipped inside and closed the doors without another glance at him. It was only once she was safely inside that she peeled back the faded curtains and watched his car drive away.

But Chelsea wasn't the only one watching Adam. Lauren, parked in her brother's black pickup down the block, was watching too. And when she caught a brief glimpse of the driver through the window, she knew exactly who he was. He was the old man's grandson. She remembered him from Greg's sentencing. He'd sat next to Mikey and wore a suit jacket and button-down shirt with no tie. That little bitch Chelsea had sat next to him.

Lauren knew then, as she knew now, that Greg would never commit armed robbery. Sure, he'd had a few brushes with the law—some drunk and disorderly charges and a DUI—but he'd never shoot someone. Not in a million years. Besides, he'd just started a new job at a plant that manufactured motorcycle parts that paid pretty decent money and found out his girlfriend, Amber, was pregnant. To throw that all away would've made no sense. Lauren sank back in her seat, thinking about the Monday before Greg's trial, when she'd confronted Chelsea about her lie.

Lauren had seethed as she aggressively maneuvered her way through the throng of students ambling down the hall. She could see Chelsea standing at her locker, back to Lauren, her long red braid snaking down her back.

"You lying piece of shit," Lauren had hissed through clenched teeth as Chelsea turned toward her. "My brother spent the night in jail because of you!"

"Lauren," Chelsea had uttered, looking around nervously as other kids began to stop and stare. "The lawyer said not to talk to you."

"I guess you'll just have to *listen*, then." Lauren had fumed, lowering her voice. "You need to go back to the lawyer and tell him he didn't rob that store."

"But he *did*. I saw him." Lauren had glared at Chelsea's perfect little turned-up nose and milky-white skin. What was she doing? Trying to convince her that Greg had tried to kill someone? She'd never felt so much hatred in her life.

"There's no way you saw him, because he said he wasn't there. Now you either made a mistake or you're lying."

"I'm not lying," Chelsea'd said, her voice strong. "Mikey said he'd already given him the money, and he shot him after that. Your *brother* did that! How can you defend him?"

"I'm not denying Mikey got shot and someone should go to jail for it, but it wasn't Greg." Chelsea had to be mistaken. There was no other rationale.

"It was him."

"Why would you try to screw us?" Lauren had asked. "I've always been cool to you." In addition to the anger and fear, Lauren had felt betrayed. She would never have considered Chelsea a friend, but she had never been an enemy, either. She and Chelsea had ended up at the same party a year prior and when one of the girls started giving her a hard time, Lauren had actually stepped in and warned the girl to stop. At the time, Chelsea had seemed grateful. It was unconscionable that Chelsea would now go out of her way to destroy Lauren's brother's life.

"The guy he robbed was in the hospital. He lost so much blood from being shot that he almost died! I'm not going to protect your brother when I know he did it," Chelsea had said. The more adamant Chelsea was, the more angry Lauren became.

"Then you're gonna pay," Lauren had threatened. "I'm the last person you wanna fuck with." If she could have gotten away with it, Lauren would have decked Chelsea right then and there, smashing her pretty little face into the metal door of the locker. But she had more self-control than that. She'd already been in trouble for assault earlier in the year and she was less than a year from graduating and getting out of the hellhole of a school she was forced to attend. Instead, she had slammed the palm of her hand against the locker next to Chelsea's face, causing her to flinch. Then she'd pushed past the students who had started to gather, and stalked off. *I can't beat the bitch up, but I can make her life unbearable. And that's my new mission.*

As Lauren took one last glance at Chelsea's mobile home and started up the engine in the truck, she smiled, proud she was responsible for making Chelsea drop out of school. There was no way anyone could have put up with what Lauren and her friends put Chelsea through. And now that Greg was about to be released, he could really make her life hell. Lauren couldn't wait.

SIX
THE KINDNESS OF STRANGERS

After tossing and turning all night, Chelsea had no choice but to drag herself out of bed and get ready for work. Jeff still hadn't called or texted and Chelsea was alternatingly mad at him for leaving her and guilty that she was somehow to blame for the current situation. Adam's question echoed through her mind. *Who leaves his pregnant girlfriend in a hotel room by herself?* Every hour that ticked by without a word from Jeff made Chelsea feel more abandoned and alone. *He can't even call me?* she fumed. Is this what their life together was going to be like? Every time they encountered a difficult situation he'd just disappear?

Luckily, unlike Jeff, Liz was already thinking about the next steps Chelsea needed to take. When she'd arrived at work, looking forward to the mindless task of scooping gelato into cups, Liz had handed her a slip of paper with the name and address of a free pregnancy clinic that was located about two miles away.

"The best thing you can do for your baby is get prenatal care right away," Liz explained. "Not only will they not charge you a penny, but they won't require your father's signature." Chelsea felt relieved. She wanted to make sure the baby was okay. She didn't mention it to Liz but she was worried about the cocktails she'd had at the Lucky Lady. If she'd known she was pregnant, she wouldn't even have been at the Lucky Lady at all. She would've been home listening to soft music and sipping caffeine-free tea. A rowdy, smoky bar wasn't an environment she wanted her kid to frequent, even if he was still curled up inside her belly.

Chelsea still wasn't showing. She'd checked in the mirror earlier when she was getting dressed for work. *It makes sense*, she'd thought. *It takes nine months to pop out a kid, there's no way I'll see a difference in twelve hours.* Although she liked the idea of having a little round pregnant tummy and showing the world she was going to be a mom, she was worried people might give her dirty looks or even say something nasty to her. People could be weird about pregnant teenagers. She'd even heard her father say from time to time that he felt bad for these young girls who got knocked up. That they had no idea how tough life would be. *Life's already tough*, Chelsea thought as she stuffed a scoop of double chocolate gelato into a cone for the customer standing in front of her. She couldn't see how a baby would make her life worse. What did she have? Pretty much nothing. She wasn't even sure if she had a boyfriend anymore. It wasn't like she had a great job that she'd have to quit. And it wasn't like she was in college and a baby would interfere with her ability to study. The night before, as she'd climbed into bed and pulled the covers over her, she had thought about all the ways a baby would make her life better. She'd finally have someone who loved her unconditionally and needed her every single day. She'd never be lonely or bored. A baby was going to bring more good to her life than not. That was going to be hard for people to understand.

Chelsea handed the man his cone, swiped his credit

card, and thanked him for coming in. Then she went back to the other side of the long counter to help the next women in line—an attractive blond woman in her thirties.

"Welcome to Stella Luna." Chelsea smiled. "I like your shirt. It's a pretty color." The woman's deep-blue V-neck chiffon blouse hung perfectly on her frame. The design was unique and the color set off her blue eyes. Chelsea had always been one to just blurt out compliments, even as a child. One of her father's favorite stories to tell was the time she was six and tried to follow a man in a white fedora into the men's room just to tell him she liked his hat.

"Oh, thanks. . . ." the woman responded, and Chelsea could tell she'd made her feel awkward. Trying to bring the focus back to gelato, she asked the woman if she'd like a sample. With forty flavors in the display and three more in the back, she had plenty to choose from.

"Actually, no. I . . ." The woman's voice trailed off for a moment as she looked around the store. Chelsea studied her, wondering if she was okay.

"I . . . I think I know what I want," the woman said,

turning back to her. "A small Cookies and Cream." The woman still seemed oddly uncomfortable, so Chelsea decided to do what she could to help her have a better day. She grabbed up a spoon but instead of digging into the Cookies and Cream, she scooped out a little bit of the pale green gelato from its tub and tucked it delicately into a sample cup. The woman stared at her.

"Coming right up," Chelsea said. "But first, you have to try this. It's the best one." She handed the sample to the woman, who took it with her left hand. Chelsea noticed how the diamond on the woman's wedding ring sparkled in the light coming through the window. The woman didn't say a word but cautiously tasted the gelato. "What do you think?" Chelsea asked, hoping she didn't hate it. "It's basil. Sounds weird but it's pretty good, huh?" The woman nodded and forced a smile, but still didn't say anything. *God, I'm making it worse*, Chelsea thought as she quickly grabbed a new spoon and began to scoop the Cookies and Cream.

"That's a pretty necklace," the woman said awkwardly, referring to the delicate gold chain adorned with a small heart-shaped pendant around Chelsea's neck. Chelsea looked up, surprised by the compliment.

"I'm guessing it had to be from your boyfriend?"

Chelsea touched the pendant, running her thumb over the tiny point at the bottom.

"No. It used to belong to my mom. My dad gave it to her on their wedding day. It's my favorite thing I own." Chelsea remembered how her father had given her the necklace after her mom passed. It had been several months since the funeral before he'd finally been able to bring himself to clean out a few of her things. As he sat on the floor of their bedroom, staring into her jewelry box, he'd cried. Chelsea remembered it vividly even though she was only seven years old. It was the only time she'd ever seen him get emotional. As he sorted through the costume bracelets, sparkly earrings, and delicate necklaces, he'd told Chelsea the story behind each piece of jewelry he'd given to her mother.

When they got to the last piece, her father pulled the heart-shaped pendant from a little pocket inside the box and delicately clasped it around her tiny neck.

"I gave this to your mom on the day we got married and I told her, I told her on that day, our last day as single people, that she'd have my heart forever," her father had said, his scruffy cheeks were wet with tears. "You came from that love, Chelsea. You were born out of the love we had for each other." Chelsea had held on to those words ever since. Whenever she was angry at her father for leaving for months at a time, or at her mother for leaving the world entirely, she thought about how she came from a place of love. *Liebe überwindet alles.*

"Gifts from mothers are special," the woman with the diamond ring said as she pulled a ten from her designer purse and slid it to Chelsea. She seemed a tiny bit more comfortable than before.

"She didn't actually give it to me," Chelsea explained. "My dad did. After she died. But she wore it every day and it makes me feel closer to her. For my next birthday, my dad said I could have her wedding ring. I'm going to put it on the same chain."

"When's your birthday?" the woman asked. She seemed more at ease and interested in making conversation.

"November," Chelsea said, looking forward to the day she could add the thin gold band.

"Let me guess. Twenty-two?"

Chelsea shook her head and smiled, used to people guessing she was much older than she was.

"I'll be *eighteen*."

The woman's hand moved to her throat and she seemed to suck in her breath a little. Chelsea was used to that as well. She half expected the woman to say what people usually did: "Wow, you're so mature," or "No way, I would've guessed you were a lot older," but she didn't say anything. And suddenly the awkward tension that was there before was back full force.

"It's four fifty," Chelsea said as she opened the register to gather the woman's change. As she handed it back, she saw the gelato was beginning to melt down the woman's hand, and quickly handed her a few napkins.

"Thank you," the woman said, and then added, "I'm sorry about your mother." Chelsea could tell she was genuinely sympathetic.

"Thank you," Chelsea replied. Believing the conversation was over, Chelsea started to turn away, so she was caught off guard when the woman asked her another question.

"Was it recent?"

"No. I only had her around for seven years of my life, and that's not a lot of time to make memories . . .

but the ones I have are really good." Chelsea wasn't sure why she added the last part. She tended to overshare. It was a habit she was trying to break, but this time, she sort of felt that the woman needed to hear it. As the door to the shop opened with a jingle and a few more customers entered, the woman dropped the quarters into the tip jar nestled next to the register and smiled.

"Thank you," the woman said.

"Have a nice day," Chelsea responded, and moved back to the other end to help the next person. She watched the woman walk out and noticed that the pretty lady in blue glanced back over her shoulder at her and smiled again. Chelsea smiled back, feeling a strange connection to her. Despite the tornado of craziness the past forty-eight hours had brought, there was just something nice about their simple exchange. Two people who would probably never see each other again found some fragile thread of commonality. *Strange how the world works*, Chelsea thought.

Five hours later, Chelsea was perched at the edge of an uncomfortable chair, waiting for her name to be called. She looked around the waiting room of the pregnancy clinic and let her gaze land on the only other patient there. The woman had short, cropped black hair, and wore a simple gray maternity shirt stretched tight over her pregnant belly. *I'm going to look like that soon*, Chelsea mused, and glanced back down at the form on her clipboard, trying not to stare. *I'm going to need to buy maternity clothes. I wonder if you can get those at the thrift store.*

Chelsea tapped the toe of her chunky platform sandals nervously up and down on the paisley carpet. The form had a box for her name and age. If she put her real name and age, would they contact her father? Liz had said they wouldn't, that everything is confidential, but Chelsea wanted to be sure. She hadn't decided when or how to break the news to her dad and she didn't want him somehow finding out from someone besides her. Hesitating, Chelsea slowly printed *Brianna Walters* in the name box and for the age, she put *19*. "Brianna" was the name of the only girlfriend her dad had that she ever liked, which unfortunately, didn't last long, and "Walters" was the last name of her favorite teacher back when she was still in school. Mr. Walters. He taught algebra and always made the students laugh, and for the first time in Chelsea's life, she actually liked going to math class.

A door leading back to the exam rooms opened and a nurse in blue scrubs stepped out.

"Denise?" the nurse said, looking down at a file. "Dr. Shollenbrook is ready to see you." The woman pushed herself up out of her chair, set her magazine aside, and disappeared into the bowels of the building. Chelsea looked back down at her form. Why so many questions? *Is this your first pregnancy? Yes. Are you under the care of another physician? No. Do you smoke? No. Do you consume alcoholic beverages? If so, how often?* Chelsea paused.

Oh god. Her thoughts flitted back to the tequila shot she'd done at the Lucky Lady. Her heart skipped a few beats. What if she'd permanently screwed up her baby because she'd been drinking? Frantically trying to do the math in her head, she counted back. How many times had she been at the Lucky Lady since she'd met Jeff? They'd known each other for a little over three months. She could've theoretically gotten pregnant the first time they'd had sex. She'd been to the bar two, maybe three times a week and had at least one drink every time she went. *Dammit*, Chelsea silently cursed herself. *I've probably had about thirty drinks.* That was thirty chances to mess up her kid. *Please don't let my baby be sick or hurt because I did that. Please, please, please let this baby be healthy.*

Yes, she checked the box. *Frequently.*

When it was Chelsea's turn to go in, a nurse handed her a plastic cup and told her they needed a urine sample to confirm her pregnancy. She gave them the sample and then went back to the waiting room again. *Maybe they'll come back and tell me I'm not pregnant, that the test Liz gave me was wrong and this is all a mistake*, she thought. Disappointment crept in at the thought. In the past twenty-four hours, she'd come to terms with the fact she was pregnant, and despite Jeff's reaction, she was excited about having a kid.

"Brianna?" the nurse said when she returned. "Come on back."

"I guess that means I'm really pregnant," Chelsea said as she followed the woman back to a room.

"You definitely are. Take everything off, put this on, opening to the front." The nurse pulled a mint-green hospital gown from the cabinet and handed it to her. "The doctor will be in soon."

Chelsea put on the gown and, pulling it tightly

around her, climbed up on the padded table covered in white paper. She looked around at the blue walls and the paintings of pregnant women. *They make pregnancy look elegant and beautiful*, she thought, as she squinted to read the artist's initials painted in the corners.

Chelsea pulled her phone from her purse and looked for a text from Jeff. Still nothing. Should she text him and tell him where she was? Would he want to be here for this? Chelsea started to compose a text: *Hey. I just wanted you to know I'm at a pregnancy clinic right now and . . .* She stopped. He'd said he needed space and she didn't want to piss him off by sending him a text too soon. And deep down, she had an inkling that even if she did tell him where she was, he wouldn't want to come meet her there. It was better not to tell him, she decided. That way, if he didn't respond to the text or if he texted back something critical, her feelings wouldn't be hurt. She tucked the phone back into her purse.

Fifteen minutes passed before the doctor, a tall African American woman, entered and introduced herself. Chelsea instantly liked her. She was calm and friendly and professional-looking. The doctor didn't congratulate her on the pregnancy, nor did she make any negative comments about Chelsea's age. She simply rolled a big white machine over and sat down on a stool.

"I'm going to do a sonogram," she explained. "It doesn't hurt at all and it allows me to see your fetus, kind of like an X-ray but completely safe for both you and the baby." Chelsea nodded and waited for the doctor to smear some cold, clear gel on her abdomen, then leaned back while Dr. Shollenbrook slid a device around as she stared at a monitor.

"Nine weeks," Dr. Shollenbrook said. "See right there? Those are the baby's feet." Dr. Shollenbrook smiled warmly and tapped a spot on the screen with her short, clean fingernail.

Chelsea studied the pulsating blob. Nothing about what the doctor pointed at even vaguely resembled feet, but Dr. Shollenbrook knew more than she did about the whole thing, so she accepted it without question.

"Cool," Chelsea replied, ready to ask the more important question. "Is it a boy or girl?"

"Still too early to know that," the doctor said and pulled the stethoscope from her ears. "At around twenty weeks we can determine the gender. We calculate your due date based on your last period."

"Oh, okay." Nine weeks. That meant she got pregnant a little over two months ago.

"Would you like to hear the heartbeat?"

Chelsea's eyes lit up. "Yeah, of course!"

Dr. Shollenbrook turned up the volume on the fetal doppler, a small plastic device that looked like a white walkie-talkie connected to a microphone. She touched the microphone end to Chelsea's belly and a faint thumping began to emanate through the tiny speaker. Chelsea smiled in awe as she listened to the rhythm of her baby's heart. After a moment, Dr. Shollenbrook sat back and asked the question Chelsea had been anticipating would come eventually.

"Does the father know that you're pregnant?"

Chelsea could feel her throat tighten. "Yes," she said without elaborating.

"Does he want to be involved?" the doctor asked gently.

"I don't really . . . I don't know." There. She said it out loud. Even though it made her feel embarrassed. *This doctor must think I'm an idiot to get pregnant with some guy who wouldn't want to be around his own baby*, she thought. But Dr. Shollenbrook didn't frown or give her a sympathetic smile. She just adjusted the back of the little gold earring in her ear and wiped the ultrasound gel from Chelsea's stomach with a paper towel.

"Are you close to your parents?"

"My mom died of cancer when I was little but I'm pretty close to my dad." Chelsea knew her father, despite his problems, would be there for her no matter what.

"Good. Well, we have resources—financial and educational—to help young women like yourself. I'll let you get dressed and then we'll go over them together, all right?"

Chelsea nodded. For the first time since she'd discovered she was pregnant, she felt like she had people in her corner who could help her. Liz and Adam were both there for her, but neither would help her support a child or show her what steps she would need to take over the next seven months. She wasn't going to go through it alone.

"Thank you," she said, truly grateful.

After the doctor pulled the door shut behind her, Chelsea sat there for a moment all by herself, her hand resting on her tummy. Her mind was still on Jeff and how she wished he were sitting beside her, holding her hand, just as excited about this baby as she was. She couldn't believe how much her life had changed in three and a half months.

SEVEN
CHANCE MEETINGS AND MARRIED MEN

The first time Chelsea saw Jeff was in the Lucky Lady. He and a friend had walked in wearing dress shirts and ties. Chelsea had been sitting at the bar, chatting with Rascal about getting her GED when she noticed them making their way over to a table in the corner. She remembered thinking about how out of place they looked in a biker bar where everyone was in worn leather jackets and sleeveless T-shirts. Chelsea had swiveled on her bar stool and watched the attractive man and his buddy as they used napkins to wipe off the chairs before they sat down, protecting their expensive slacks.

Attractive Guy's friend, a slightly chubby, clean-shaven man had walked up to the bar and waved at Rascal.

"We'll take a pitcher of whatever domestic you have on tap," he'd said as he unbuttoned the top button of his collared shirt. He seemed to relax a little once that button was undone.

"Twelve bucks," Rascal said. The guy handed him a gold credit card.

"Keep it open." Rascal slipped the card into the register drawer.

"I'll bring it over in a minute." The guy nodded and headed back over to the table under a neon Stoli sign that illuminated the window above their heads.

When the pitcher was finished filling with foamy amber beer, Rascal set it on the counter along with two clean glasses.

"Take that over to those suits for me, would ya?" he asked. Chelsea, glad to have something to do, slipped off her stool and walked slowly across the room, careful not to spill even a drop.

"Bartender asked me to bring this over." Chelsea smiled as she set the glasses down. As she looked up, she remembered Attractive Guy giving her an impressed look—the kind guys give when they want a girl to know they're intrigued. He didn't say anything, though.

"Thanks," his friend said.

Chelsea walked back to her seat at the bar. As she hopped up onto the stool, she glanced over her shoulder and noticed that Attractive Guy was still eyeing her as his friend poured beer into the glasses.

For the next half hour, Chelsea hoped he would come over to talk to her, but he didn't. A few times she thought about walking over to his table, sitting down, and striking up a conversation, but she couldn't bring herself to do that. Tired of the noise, Chelsea eventually went outside for some fresh air.

Chelsea plopped down on the curb away from the entrance. Pulling out her cell phone, she dialed her father's number. He had been gone for almost a week, working for some guy who needed help laying carpet in a motel in Iowa, and she missed him. She felt a surge of disappointment when his voice came on the line in a tinny recording. *You've reached Dom. Leave a message.*

"Hi, Dad. Everything's fine here. Just calling to say hi. I love you. Call me when you can." She wondered if he was sitting in some dive bar in a depressed area of Des Moines, sucking back whiskey and flirting with women who were impressed by motorcycles.

"You okay?" a deep, masculine voice asked. Chelsea looked up to see Attractive Guy walking toward her from the parking lot. She was surprised to see him out there and even more surprised that he was finally talking to her.

"I'm fine. My brain needed a little silence," she replied, tucking her phone back into her pocket. She had no more than finished her sentence when a car horn blared from the nearby street. She smiled at the irony and Attractive Guy did too.

"Not sure you're going to find that out here, either." He grinned as he stepped toward her. She smiled and shrugged. "Forgive me for saying this, but you don't seem like you really fit in with the crowd here. . . ." He nodded toward the entrance.

"I thought the same about you and your friend," she replied, making a point to look at his silk necktie that now hung loosely around his neck.

"Orin. We stopped for gas up the road. Saw this place and thought we'd check it out."

"Orin's a cool name." She'd never heard it before.

"What about you? Do you have a cool name?" he asked flirtatiously.

“Chelsea. And you are . . . ?”

“Jeff. Plain old Jeff.”

“Except not that plain and not that old.” She flirted back, liking the attention. Jeff chuckled. She could tell he appreciated the compliment. He was tall and attractive and she liked that he wasn’t trying to hang all over her.

“Can I sit?” he asked, racking up another point in his favor. Most guys just assumed they could take the seat next to her without asking.

“You’re gonna get your pants dirty,” she warned, remembering how he’d wiped off the chair before sitting inside.

“I don’t mind,” he said, and sat down next to her, resting his elbows on his knees. “I’m still trying to figure out what you’re doing out here alone.”

“What’s wrong with doing things by yourself?” She leaned in as she asked, looking into his eyes. She spent the majority of her time alone. Although it was lonely at times, especially when her father was away on long trips, being by herself actually made her feel calm and centered. Better to be alone than in bad company.

“Nothing. It just doesn’t seem . . .” His voice trailed off as he rephrased his thought. “I would think the guys in there would be all over you." *Plain old Jeff is right about that*, she thought. *They usually are, and it's annoying.*

"They're not my type," she responded firmly, not one hundred percent sure she knew what her type was. Whatever it was, it certainly did not hang out at the Lucky Lady.

Jeff seemed to want to say something but then changed his mind. Instead he pointed to the tattoo on the inside of her ankle written in German. "'Love conquers all.' Is that right?"

"*Ja!*" she said, impressed. No one ever knew what that meant. "*Sprechen Sie Deutsch?*"

"*Ein bisschen*," he replied with good pronunciation. "I took a few years in high school." She smiled, feeling a little closer to him.

"It was my mother's favorite saying," she explained, as she had so many times before when people asked about it. "She was from Düsseldorf. I've never been there but I've seen pictures and it's beautiful." Jeff studied her for a moment.

"You get more interesting by the minute," he said softly. Before he could say anything more, Orin poked his head out the door.

"Hey, man . . . you find your wallet?" Orin asked. Jeff quickly stood up like a child caught with his hand in the cookie jar. He pulled his wallet from his pocket. For the first time, she noticed the gold wedding band on his left ring finger. It had been there the whole time, obviously, but she hadn't seen it. Or maybe she hadn't wanted to see it.

"Left it in the car." Chelsea saw Orin look from Jeff to her and then back to Jeff before raising his eyebrow in disapproval. Then Orin went back inside.

"Why the poisonous stare?" Chelsea asked, not sure she understood the silent exchange that had just taken place.

"He probably thinks I made up the wallet thing just to come out here and talk to you."

"Did you?"

"No, but when I saw you sitting here, I wasn't going to pass up an opportunity." She smiled, flattered. "It was nice talking to you, Chelsea," Jeff said as he stuffed his wallet back into his dark gray slacks. She remained seated, wishing he didn't feel the need to go.

"If you want to talk to me again, you can." She wasn't entirely sure what made her say it. She hadn't really thought about dating him or pursuing any sort of relationship. And she knew the chances of a professional, married guy wanting to date her were slim. He probably had a gorgeous wife and some nice, big house on a tree-lined street. No way could she compete with that. But she liked his company and they had a lot in common. Maybe they could kill time together. Chatting with Jeff under the starry night sky, speaking in her mother's native language, was better than sitting alone in a dank bar.

Jeff paused, looked around uncomfortably, then pulled his business card from his pocket. "Here's my information. . . . I'll leave that up to you."

Chelsea looked down at the card: Jeff Clefton. He was the vice president of sales for Carrus Furnishings. Chelsea had never heard of the company but figured it was probably pretty big. His cell phone number was printed in glossy black type under his name. Chelsea smiled.

"*Guten nacht*," she said, telling him "good night" in German.

"*Guten nacht*," he replied, before grinning awkwardly and walking back into the bar.

A few days later, Chelsea, all alone and bored, had decided to call him.

"Hi, is this Jeff?" she said when she heard him answer her call.

"Yes, who's this?" he asked, not recognizing her voice.

"Chelsea. *Wie gehts?*" She decided to ask how he was doing in German to spark his memory.

"Chelsea, hi," he said. "Hang on a minute." The line went silent and when he came back on, he seemed lighter, happier than before. "I'm glad you called."

"Are you busy? Did I catch you at a bad time?" She suddenly felt nervous.

"Not at all. I just needed to get off the other line."

"Oh. Okay. Well, I didn't really have a reason for calling. I just wanted to tell you that I enjoyed our conversation the other night."

"So did I. Would you like to . . . maybe continue it over lunch?" Was he asking her on a date? Or was it just a friendly get-together? Either way, she wanted to do it.

The following day they met for lunch at a bistro a few blocks from Stella Luna. It was at that lunch, over Caesar salads and turkey paninis, that Chelsea realized Jeff was like no one she'd ever known. He was classy and smart and funny, and he seemed to like her the way she wanted to be liked. He had done most of the talking, which made it easy. She didn't have to reveal anything about where she lived or the fact she'd dropped out of high school, or explain where her father was. Those facts were embarrassing. She used to mention them, but it didn't take long to realize people judged her because of them. They either felt she was just poor white trash going nowhere with her life, or they felt sorry for her. She didn't want Jeff to do either one.

Jeff told her about the company he worked for and a few funny stories about Orin and how he loved to ski and tried to get out to Tahoe or Aspen at least once a year. He'd even been to Europe a few times. Never Germany, only France, England, and Portugal. But still, it was much closer than she'd ever been. He had not mentioned his wife at all, and Chelsea, at least on that first lunch meeting, never asked.

EIGHT
MONEY MATTERS

It was dark by the time Chelsea stepped off the bus at the corner of 147th and Maytag and began the four-block walk home. As she made her way along the broken sidewalk, she thought about the parenting class she sat in on. Dr. Shollenbrook had told her that they were offering free classes at the community center next door and invited her to stay and check it out. She had killed a few hours at a coffee shop, and then took the refill of green tea with her as she walked down to the large brick building with mirrored windows.

The teacher was a pretty African American woman

with bright red lipstick, and Chelsea liked listening to her.

"We all know babies do three things: they eat, sleep, and poop. Last week we covered sleeping and pooping, and tonight we'll cover eating. This is an important one cuz as soon as that kid pops out, it's gonna be hungry." The students, mostly women and men a little older than Chelsea, laughed. Chelsea laughed too. Taking care of a baby didn't sound scary, the way Red Lipstick Lady told it. She made it sound logical and easy, and even fun. The way Mr. Walters made math class fun.

Afterward, Chelsea scooped up every pamphlet on parenting they'd set out on the scratched wooden table in the front of the room, figuring she could read more about parenting and what the community center offered in her spare time. She couldn't wait to go back and learn some more. Thinking about the class brought a smile to her face, which quickly faded as she turned the corner and spotted a familiar car parked in front of her house. Jeff's Mercedes. Her heart fluttered for a moment. Why was he there waiting for her? Had he come by to apologize and say he wanted to be a real father to their kid? She hoped so.

When he saw her, he got out of his car and met her in the street.

"Chelsea," he said calmly.

"Hi." She felt the need to be cautious even though she really wanted to throw her arms around him the way she'd done before. "I thought you were going to call me."

"Better to talk in person when it's something important." She nodded and led him into the mobile home. Jeff took a seat at the kitchen table as Chelsea put her backpack down.

"You want coffee or something?" she asked. His demeanor was strained and he shook his head.

"No thanks. We need to talk about this situation."

"Situation"? Didn't he mean "baby"? Shouldn't they be talking about their child? Chelsea filled a kettle full of water from the faucet and set it on the stove for tea. She turned around and leaned back against the counter. "Have you thought about what you want to do?"

"I don't understand the question." What she wanted to do? Wasn't it clear she wanted to marry him and raise their kid like normal people?

"Have you thought . . ." he said in a frustrated tone before calming himself and continuing, ". . . about having an abortion?"

"No," she said adamantly. "No way. I'm excited about being a mom." After what she'd learned today at her appointment and the parenting class, she had an even clearer understanding of why she wanted to be a mother than she'd had before.

"You're seventeen, Chelsea! Why on earth do you think it's a good idea to keep this baby?"

"Because I love you and I love this child."

"But I don't want to have a kid with you. I can't."

Chelsea felt like she had been punched in the gut. She couldn't believe what Jeff was saying. Didn't he love her? A few days ago, they'd been talking about how they'd be together after his divorce and now he was telling her he didn't want his kid?

"The kid is coming, though," she said, still trying to wrap her head around what he meant. Did he think she was too immature to be a good mother? Did she just need to prove to him that she was ready?

"I can do this," she continued. "I know you think I can't because I'm too young, but I can. I even started parenting classes today. I'll learn everything I need to know." Jeff heaved a loud, dismissive sigh.

"You are a high school dropout, Chelsea. How are you going to support this baby on a minimum-wage job? You don't have a real income!" She ignored his condescending tone.

"But you do."

"Oh good god," Jeff said in an exasperated tone and ran his fingers through his hair.

"You have money and I can give the baby love. That's more than most people have. It's more than I had. We never had money." Why was he having so much trouble believing she could make it work? He knocked his knuckles angrily against the top of the table.

"I can't financially support a child if I'm in *jail.* And that's exactly where I'll be if anyone finds out I got a seventeen-year-old pregnant." Who said anything about jail? Yes, she was underage, but it wasn't like he raped her. They were in love. The sex was consensual and so what if he was quite a bit older than she was? If it didn't matter to her, why should it matter to anyone else?

"It won't be that way" was all she could think to say.

"Listen to me!" He raised his voice. "I need you to understand the situation I'm in. I talked to a lawyer. They will charge me as a *sex offender*. I'll lose my job. I'll never be allowed to even get near the child. This is not the life you or I want."

"I'll be eighteen before the baby's born."

"It doesn't matter!" He sneered.

"Fine! I won't put your name on the birth certificate. There!"

"You aren't hearing me. I don't want to be with you. I don't want to marry you and I can't have anything to do with this baby."

"But you said after your divorce—"

"That was before I knew how old you are. Seventeen! Christ. You're a child. Even if you were of age, what are people going to say when they see us together? My family? The people I work with? There's no way this is ever going to work. It just isn't."

"But we love each other and—"

"Jesus!" Jeff interrupted. "Just stop with all your ethereal, whimsical, happy-go-lucky bullshit! This is the real world! Love does *not* conquer all!" Tears welled in Chelsea's eyes. She was utterly confused about how much of what he was saying was true. *Is this what he really thinks of me?* she wondered. He'd said countless times that he loved her because she was so free, so spontaneous, so undaunted by all the things in the world that make people jaded and unable to trust. Now he was using all of that against her.

"Listen to me," he said softly, and pulled a plain white envelope from his jacket pocket. He slid it toward her. "I want what's best for both of us. There's ten thousand dollars in there. If you let me take you to get an abortion, it's all yours. You can use it to go to Germany or move out . . . or anything you want." Chelsea looked up at him, surprised. Ten thousand dollars. How could he put a price on his own child? "I'm not trying to buy you off," he continued. "It's only fair that if you give me what I want, you get something out of it too." Chelsea stared at the envelope, incensed.

"I want this baby. I *need* this baby. I'd never force you to be a part of its life. I won't tell anyone that you're the father." There! She solved all his problems. She'd keep the paternity of the baby secret. "I have nothing! Except my dad who's never around. I don't have a career . . . or an education . . . but I have a baby growing inside of me. A *real* baby. With a heartbeat and little feet. Do you know what that makes me? It makes me a mom. It makes me important to someone!" The words came out with such force, Chelsea surprised herself. "There is no way in hell I'm giving this baby up. No abortion. No adoption. It stays with me!"

He just stared at her. She could tell he wasn't expecting her to take a stand. Then, suddenly, Jeff stood up, grabbed the envelope and smacked it down on the table in front of her. Chelsea jumped, shocked by the sudden display of aggression.

"Don't be stupid! Take the fucking money! You're young! You can have ten more kids down the line if you want. You will never have ten thousand dollars cash again!"

Chelsea couldn't believe what she was hearing. She'd never seen this side of him before—the side that thinks he can buy off people whenever he wants. If he was trying to intimidate her, she wasn't going to let it work. Grabbing the envelope, she whisked past Jeff and marched out the front door. As he came out after her, she threw the envelope into the night sky and the money scattered across the scrubby patch of grass that made up her front yard.

"I don't want your money!" she yelled. "I'm keeping

this baby and if you don't want to be a part of its life, get out!" Chelsea didn't normally air her dirty laundry in front of the neighbors, but she was so angry, she didn't care. She wanted Jeff gone. He started to frantically collect the twenty-dollar bills that the breeze had carried down the sidewalk as Chelsea entered the trailer and slammed the door.

So I guess Chelsea received some interesting news at the pregnancy clinic, Lauren mused as she sat in her brother's truck observing the attractive man in his business suit scrambling to pick up the cascading cash. Although she was parked almost a block away, she had heard everything through her open window.

What a break! The hours of boring surveillance had finally paid off. This was better than a soap opera; the pregnant teen taking a stand against her rich older boyfriend who wants her to get rid of her baby. Dramatic! *He certainly looks rich*, Lauren thought. Those threads he had on cost a pretty penny and from the looks of it, there was quite a bit of money in that envelope. The brand-new shiny Mercedes, completely out of place in this neighborhood, sealed the deal for Lauren. *Greg's going to die when he hears about this*, she thought as she watched the man hurl the envelope onto the passenger seat and get into his car.

Lauren reveled in playing detective. This was the kind of discovery that would make Greg proud. After all, it had been almost two weeks since he'd asked her to tail Chelsea and find out as much as she could about her, and this was the first interesting thing that she'd witnessed. She needed to gather information about Daddy Warbucks. The more she knew about him, the more she knew about Chelsea.

The Mercedes's taillights finally came on and Lauren started her engine. The man's car drove off down the street, on its way to a better part of town. Lauren stayed close behind. If there was a way to get back at Chelsea, perhaps her baby daddy was the key. And to know more about him, she'd need his name. And to get that, she'd need to follow him all the way home.

The unexpected confrontation with Jeff left Chelsea rattled. Jeff didn't love her or want to be with her. That was clear. Her heart ached thinking about it. She loved him—at least she thought she did. After what just happened, she wasn't so sure. But her relationship with Jeff was nothing compared to the doubt Jeff had planted in her mind about her ability to raise a kid.

The parenting class and visit with Dr. Shollenbrook had made Chelsea believe that she really could be a good mother at her age, but now she couldn't help but wonder if Jeff was right. She didn't have a job that would allow her to afford everything a baby needed, and the fact that Jeff wasn't willing to be involved in any way, or even admit the child was his, infuriated her. At the very least, the baby needed him financially. She'd really thought that Jeff would eventually come around and be as excited about the pregnancy as she was. Now she couldn't even name him on the birth certificate. *My child isn't going to know who his father is.* The thought tied her stomach in knots. *He deserves to have a dad to look up to, to play with, to love.* Maybe she hadn't had the best father in the world, but she'd never doubted how much he loved her. And the memories she had with him—reading her bedtime stories and taking her to the county fair—she treasured them. Her child would never have an opportunity to know what that was like. Was she making the wrong decision? Should she give this baby up? The thought terrified her.

No, she thought. *Where there's a will, there's a way.*

Deep down, there was one thing she was now sure of. She would be a good mother. And there was one thing she now knew that she hadn't before—Jeff was a liar. He'd lied about loving her and wanting to be with her. And she wasn't going to trust anything he said ever again. *I'm not going to let him intimidate me into doing what's best for him.* She needed to do what was best for her and the baby. If Jeff really loved her, he'd want the same.

Chelsea pulled a battered, dust-laden box from the top shelf of her father's closet and sat down on the floor. She opened the flaps and peered into the box, hit by the smell of mildew. Pulling out some old drawings she made in elementary school, Chelsea found what she was looking for: her old baby things.

She removed a pair of yellowing booties and some infant clothes, but kept digging until she saw the baby book her mother made. Delicately lifting it from the box, Chelsea opened the fragile cover to see a lock of her red hair taped to the first page. Under it, in German, her mother had written *The lock of hair Chelsea was born with.* Tears began to stream down Chelsea's cheeks and she didn't bother to try to hold them in. As she slowly turned the page, she saw a photo of her mother holding her on the day she was born. Her mother, tucked into her hospital bed, wearing a light blue hospital gown, smiled brightly at the camera, baby Chelsea in her arms.

"I need you so much right now, Mom," Chelsea whispered longingly at the photo. "I need you *so much.*"

Chelsea tried hard to conjure up her earliest memory of her mother, but it was the last day they had together that came to mind. The small room with green walls and yellow curtains that billowed as the March breeze drifted in.

"Are you cold, Mom?" Chelsea had asked, perched on the edge of a chair pulled up to her mother's hospice bed. Her mother barely moved as she shook her head. The woman lying there only vaguely resembled the cheery, bubbly spitfire of a woman she'd known. Her bright red hair had mostly fallen out and her eyes looked dull and hollow. When Chelsea held her mother's hand, it felt weak and cold, and she was afraid if she squeezed too hard, she might break it.

"When I get better . . ." her mother had said in a raspy voice, "we'll fly that kite you made. Daddy can drive us up to Fairmount Park. And we can see the cherry blossoms." The words came out uneven and Chelsea knew it took all her mother's energy to talk. Her mother said it as if she believed she'd somehow beat the cancer that had taken over nearly every organ in her body. At the time, Chelsea, only seven years old, nodded, holding on to hope that her mother would eventually get better and they would indeed fly the flimsy blue-and-orange kite she'd made with tissue paper and tongue depressors above the pink blooms of the cherry blossom trees.

"I love you, Mama," Chelsea had said, and rested her head on her mother's pillow.

"*Ich liebe dich auch*, *schnucki*," she said back, which Chelsea knew meant "I love you too, sweetie." Her voice was almost inaudible. "Go home with Daddy now. I'll see you tomorrow."

Chelsea had kissed her mother on the cheek and gathered up her backpack and the school books she'd brought to read to her sick mother. As she walked out the door to find her father who had gone to talk to a nurse, she took one last look at her mother. All she could see was her bony shoulder in a flannel nightgown jutting up over the blankets, and the side of her mother's pale face.

The next day, when her father picked her up from

school Chelsea asked, "Are we going to see Mom? I made her this." Chelsea held up a picture she'd drawn of a butterfly. "I even wrote the word for butterfly in German. Did I spell it right?" *Schmetterling.* Her father nodded even though he hadn't looked at it.

"No, we're going home," he said, and her stomach dropped. Even at that tender age, she knew her mother hadn't recovered enough to be sent home.

"Why?" she asked anyway, already knowing the answer.

"Because your mom's not at the hospice house anymore. The angels came last night and took her to heaven." Just like that, she was gone.

The ring of Chelsea's cell phone brought her back to the present, forcing her to let go of her mother like she'd done so many times before. Chelsea looked down at the phone. It was Adam. Her heart skipped.

"Hello?" she answered, worried that he'd hear the sadness in her voice and begin to think that all she ever does is cry.

"I'm a dick," Adam said lightly. Chelsea couldn't help but smile a little. She had no clue what he was referring to, but he sounded remorseful. She was just glad to hear his husky voice.

"What do you mean?"

"I gave you a hard time about being with that douchebag and . . . I had no right to do that. It actually meant a lot that you opened up to me about all that." She could hear him swallow on the other end and knew he was eating. It made her feel like things with Adam were back to normal. She pictured him sitting in the back room of Mikey's store scooping cereal out of a bowl with a plastic spoon.

"You were right. He doesn't care about me or the baby and he doesn't want to be with me. I'm a complete idiot for even getting involved with him." She decided not to mention that Jeff had tried to buy her off with ten grand.

"He lied to you. You didn't know."

"I just don't want this baby to be a bad thing. I want it to be something beautiful, because it is." It felt so natural to talk to Adam. The words came out exactly the way she wanted them to.

"I don't doubt that if anyone could give a child love, it's you."

"I feel so alone. I wish my dad was here," Chelsea said, not even realizing she'd said it. Adam's faith in her made her feel like she could admit this to him, though.

"Can I come over and cheer you up?" Adam asked. Without thinking, Chelsea brought her fingertip to her lip. Every part of her wanted Adam there but she suddenly felt nervous.

"Um, yeah, okay," she said, and began to tuck the items on the floor back into the box.

"Are you sure? If you'd rather be alone, that's cool too." He was giving her an out, but Chelsea pushed her nerves aside. She wasn't sure why seeing Adam again caused this strange anxiety. It wasn't bad, it was just weird. Maybe it was because she'd told him so much. Now she felt vulnerable. And yet, the idea of him sitting next to her, smiling, made her calm. She definitely needed that.

"Yes, I want you to come over."

"Great," he said. "See you in a little bit."

Chelsea ended the call and got to her feet. She went into the bathroom to check her appearance. *I look terrible*, she concluded, studying her red, puffy eyes. She'd cried so much in the past couple of days, it seemed like her eyes might stay that way permanently. Squirting face wash into her hand, she smeared it all over her face and worked it into a lather. Then she turned on the warm water and rinsed it all off. *That's better*, she thought. At least she could put on some makeup to hide the dark circles and the smattering of acne on her jaw line. *I never get zits. It must be from the pregnancy.* If she did her hair just right, she could kind of cover them. At least enough that Adam might not notice.

An hour later, Adam was sitting across from her at the kitchen table, his jacket slung over the chair, his hair still damp from a shower. It fell over his ears in short black ringlets. An assortment of Chinese takeout boxes were spread between them. Chelsea, feeling more presentable in black mascara and shimmery lip gloss, nabbed up a chunk of sweet and sour pork and popped it into her mouth. Her mood was much lighter now.

"I'm not trying that one. Ever," she said, poking at the box full of braised chicken feet.

"It's good." Adam laughed, his eyes sparkling. "You eat chicken legs, don't you? What's wrong with the feet?" Chelsea dug one out with her chopsticks and made it slowly scratch Adam's forearm with its hooked toenail.

"What is this? A toenail? A claw? What do chickens have?"

He laughed and pulled his thick arm away, wiping

off the trail of syrupy sauce with his napkin.

"They have feet, so it must be a toenail. To have a claw, it needs to have a paw. Hey that rhymed." He smiled proudly.

"The doctor specifically told me not to eat this." Chelsea waved the foot from side to side. "She said it would screw up the baby."

"She did not!" Adam laughed even harder. It was a deep, infectious laugh that he'd had since he was a kid. "Come on, Chelsea. Be brave!" Chelsea grinned and brought the foot to her mouth dramatically as if she might eat it. She could see Adam was impressed. Closing her eyes, she took a bite of the chicken foot, mulled it around in her mouth, and spit it back into her hand.

"Holy crap, that's disgusting!" she blurted out as Adam laughed hysterically. "I did it, though. Don't ever call me a chicken!"

He laughed as she wiped her mouth in an attempt to get rid of the taste, before tucking back into his food. Chelsea could sense the moment turning serious when Adam glanced up at her and lightly bit his bottom lip. Something about the way he looked at her made her feel tingly.

"You are one of the bravest people I know," he said, locking eyes with her. She had a hard time looking away. "I mean it. What you did for my grandpa when you testified back then . . . I know you were scared but you did it anyway. And I'll never forget that."

"Thanks," Chelsea said quietly, reminded that Greg Foster was getting out. It had only been three days since Mikey told her the news about Greg's parole but it seemed like months. She thought back to the day she had climbed up on the stand in that huge courtroom downtown and testified. She had been so terrified and anxious, but she'd mustered the courage to climb into the witness stand, believing he'd go away for a long time. "It doesn't matter, though, right? He'll be back on the streets next week."

"It does matter, though." Adam leaned closer. Chelsea could feel his leg press against hers under the table. "The fact you did that, you made a stand for Grandpa, is what kept him going."

"What do you mean?" she asked.

"When he found out he was going to have to use a cane for the rest of his life, he got really . . . I don't know, despondent." Adam's features darkened. "Didn't want to see anyone, didn't want to go out and do anything . . . we were all super worried about him. But when you told him you'd testify, it changed all that. It was like he had to get better so that you wouldn't be doing that for nothing. Does that make sense?" It was the first time Chelsea had heard that about Mikey. She had no idea that she had given him hope. She just wanted to see someone who hurt a person she cared about behind bars.

"You'll get through this too," Adam assured her, and placed his hand on hers. She felt her cheeks grow hot, her gaze lost in his. "You don't need some successful business-troll like Jeff to help you, either. You're a tough little thing."

"Do you really think so?" She needed to hear him say it again. Not just anyone, but him. She knew Adam would never tell her something that wasn't true.

"Yes. I know so." A moment passed between them like she'd never felt before. Not with Jeff, or any other guy. For a brief second, it felt like they were the only two people on earth. She wanted him to lean in and kiss her. She wanted to feel the touch of his lips against hers. She wanted to taste him. *He must not want to*, she thought as Adam suddenly looked away, his face crimson. He spotted a deck of cards on the side table and picked them up. Chelsea exhaled, long and slow, trying to play off the disappointment she felt.

"Know how to play Ninety-nine?" he asked, his voice tense. She'd never even heard of the game.

"No," she said quietly.

"I'll teach you."

NINE
TIT FOR TAT

"What'd you find out?" Greg plopped down across from Lauren. *He looks good*, Lauren thought. Better than the last time she'd come to visit. He'd lost a little weight, but he seemed more muscular, even under his faded orange jumpsuit. He certainly looked better than a lot of the inmates seated at other tables in the room, speaking softly to their visitors.

"A bunch of stuff," she gushed, barely able to contain her excitement. "But here's the kicker. Yesterday, she went to a pregnancy clinic, so she's knocked up."

"Really?" her brother murmured, intrigued.

"Wait. It gets better. When she got home last night, she had a huge fight with some rich guy who has a Mercedes. I think he's the father and was trying to buy her off to get an abortion. She threw an envelope at him that had a shitload of money in it."

"You saw the money?" Greg leaned in.

"Uh, yeah. It flew all over. He was scrambling to pick it all back up without getting his nice suit dirty." Lauren laughed, picturing it in her mind. Greg smiled.

"You did good, little sis." Lauren beamed, happy that she'd proven herself. "I'm thinking *possibilities* right now."

"I just want revenge. Look how much you've suffered . . . how much Mom has suffered because of her." They'd barely been holding on to begin with. Ever since their father left, Greg had been the one to keep the family together. Their mother wasn't good at taking care of herself, or anyone else for that matter, and Greg was the one who handled everything from finances to protecting Lauren from the creepers who lived in their neighborhood.

"Gelato Bitch can't make things right but her rich

sugar daddy can." Greg smirked.

"Restitution?" Lauren asked, wondering what Greg had in mind.

"Restitution."

TEN
UNEXPECTED ENCOUNTERS

This is cute, Chelsea thought as she held up a green-and-white onesie in size 0–3 months. Damn, six dollars for that? It was *used.* How could something so small cost almost as much as one of her own shirts? Chelsea hung the onesie back on the rack and continued to peruse the aisle of the thrift store, hoping to find some baby clothes that cost two dollars or less. After Adam had gone home the night before, she'd started to put together a budget for the baby and realized if she could just save two dollars per day, she'd have $430 by the time the baby was born to spend on diapers, food, clothes, and formula. The hard thing would be the expensive stuff like a crib and stroller and high chair. Maybe if she checked the free ads each Saturday, she'd be able to find someone who was willing to give that stuff away. As Chelsea spotted a plain white onesie for only a dollar, she heard a familiar voice.

"Oh. Hey. I remember you." Chelsea looked up to see the woman who had asked her about her necklace in the gelato shop step up next to her. "You work down the street. Basil gelato." Chelsea remembered her instantly. *What was she doing in a thrift store?* Chelsea wondered as she took in the woman's flowing pink shirt and designer jeans. This woman clearly had enough to buy beautiful, expensive clothes. Regardless, Chelsea was happy to see her again. Their conversation on the day after Chelsea had found out she was pregnant had been a high point in an otherwise stressful day.

"This baby stuff is so cute," the woman said, pulling a lacy pink dress from the rack. "I wish I could buy all of it."

"You have a baby?" Chelsea asked, intrigued.

"No. I just love kids. How 'bout you?" the woman asked. Chelsea nodded, proud.

"I'm expecting." *Expecting*. It was the first time

she'd used that word and she was surprised how special and important it made her feel.

"Congratulations." The woman smiled, but it seemed forced. "Have you picked out a name yet?"

"No, not yet," Chelsea responded. She hadn't even started thinking about names. "Any ideas? I'm open to suggestions."

"For a boy, Alexander. And for a girl, Annette," the woman replied without hesitation.

"Both As. They'll always be the first ones when the teacher tells them to line up."

"I never thought of that." The woman seemed more relaxed now. "Alexander was my grandfather's name and Annette was my grandmother's."

"People don't do that as much anymore . . . name kids after family members. . . ."

"No, they don't. How about your boyfriend or husband? Does he have an opinion?" Boyfriend or husband. Jeff was neither and given that he didn't want her to keep the baby, she was pretty sure he didn't give a flying crap about its name.

"We're not really . . . *together* anymore. So it'll just be up to me."

"I'm sorry to hear that." The woman seemed a little surprised but genuinely sorry.

"It happens," Chelsea said with a shrug. "I know I'm still gonna be a really good mom. I started a parenting class already."

"Oh really? Where?"

"Billauer Community Center. They teach you basically everything you need to know." The woman smiled but seemed to be lost in thought. There was something so warm about this lady, and yet a bit odd. Chelsea couldn't put her finger on it.

"Are you okay?" Chelsea asked.

"Yes, of course." She smiled, but it didn't seem genuine. It looked like the kind of smile that is supposed to tell the world things are fine when they really aren't.

"I better get back," Chelsea said, stealing a glance at her phone. "My lunch break is almost over." The woman nodded politely. Chelsea walked toward the exit, deciding to come back when she had more time to shop. As she opened the door and stepped out into the blinding sunlight, she looked back inside, curious if the lady was still looking at baby clothes. But the woman was gone.

* * *

Back at home, Chelsea stood in front of her closet, staring at the simple black dress she'd worn so many times on nights out with Jeff and wondering if it would be appropriate for tonight. Adam had texted her as she neared the end of her shift: *Would you like to go out to dinner with me tonight?*

She had said yes, and then immediately started wondering what his invitation meant. Was that just a casual sequel to last night's Chinese takeout? Or did he mean it to be like a date?

Chelsea heaved a sigh as she thought about Adam. She kept picturing that shock of black hair that never seemed to stay in place and the way his thin cotton T-shirt fell over his shoulders, defining every muscle. She had felt drawn to Adam before, but never with this kind of intensity. She wondered if it was the pregnancy hormones. Or perhaps it was because she was on the rebound from Jeff, in desperate need for someone to show her some affection.

But it seemed like more than that. After the events of the last few days, she realized that she felt so much more grounded with Adam than she did with Jeff. When she thought about Adam, she found herself smiling. It hadn't been that way with Jeff. When Jeff wasn't with her, she had constantly been worried about the next time he would call or if he'd changed his mind about divorcing his wife. There was a feeling of excitement with Jeff, but never calm. She wondered if maybe she'd confused love with a desire for a white knight who would scoop her up and give her a better life than the one she had.

When she was with Adam, her current life didn't seem so bad. He knew exactly who she was, and she knew him, and there was something comforting in that, something that just felt natural.

This is probably not a date, she thought as she ran her finger over the collar of the black dress. Why would Adam—or any guy—want to be with a girl who was having someone else's kid? *That's my new reality. I'm probably going to be single for a very long time. That's fine, though*, she told herself. She wouldn't be alone—she had her baby. It would take up so much of her time she wouldn't have room in her life for a boyfriend. Boyfriends leave, anyway. Her child would be there forever. Her thoughts drifted back to the dress. *Wherever he takes me, this dress will be fine*, she decided. Even if it was too dressy, at least he'd know she'd put some effort into it.

As it turned out, the dress wasn't too dressy at all. Adam had surprised her when he came to her door wearing a suit jacket over a crisp white shirt. He looked incredible. He also carried a little bouquet of yellow daisies wrapped in plastic.

"Hi," he said. She could tell he was nervous. "These are for you." He stretched his arm out to hand her the flowers. She gently took them.

"What are these for?" she asked without thinking.

"Just to brighten up the room."

"Thank you," she said, and opened the door wider so he could come in. "They're so pretty." She inhaled their fresh scent.

"You can leave 'em in the fridge until you get back if you want. The lady said that would be fine."

"Okay." Chelsea opened the refrigerator and delicately placed the bouquet on the top shelf. When she turned back to Adam, he was awkwardly shifting his weight from side to side.

"Are you ready?" he asked.

"Sure." She slipped her purse strap over her shoulder and grabbed her jacket. "Where are we going?"

"It's a surprise. But you'll like it."

Adam's car pulled to the curb in front of Locanda Postino, an intimate little hole-in-the-wall on a quaint street in the arts district. From the outside it didn't look like much, but the interior was beautifully upscale. Its crushed-velvet seats and the gold-painted Venetian masks with their long hooked noses that lined the walls made Chelsea feel like she'd been magically transported to Italy. Even the waiter had an Italian accent.

"This restaurant is expensive," Chelsea whispered as she glanced at the menu. Some of the dishes cost more than she spent on groceries in a week. What was osso bucco? Whatever it was, it was pricey. Nervous, she tapped the stem of her water glass with her finger. Adam lifted his gaze and smiled. She immediately felt at ease.

"There's no budget tonight. Gramps chose this place and he gave me his credit card," Adam said firmly, flipping the page. "The puttanesca sounds good."

"Really?" She was surprised Mikey even knew about it.

"Are you kidding? He was thrilled when I told him I was taking you on a date."

"This is a *date*?" she asked, caught off guard by

the word. As soon as she said it, she could see Adam retract uncomfortably and she regretted not keeping her mouth shut.

"Isn't it? I mean, no pressure if you don't want it to be but . . . this is my best tie so . . . I was thinking it was. . . ." Adam grinned to lighten the conversation and gestured to his tie, which sported little blue geometric designs.

"Why would you want to date a pregnant girl?" she blurted out. Adam set his sparkling water down, thrown.

"Huh?" he said, and looked around to make sure no one was eavesdropping.

Chelsea lowered her voice. "I'm serious. It doesn't make sense."

Adam pondered the question for a moment and exhaled before answering. "Well, I don't really think of you as a pregnant girl. I think of you as this girl Chelsea I've liked for a long time." Chelsea took in his words. They were genuine, as always. She was impressed that he could put himself out there like that. Adam never seemed scared of rejection. She liked that. There were a lot of things about him that she liked. But it still didn't make sense to her that he could overlook the fact she was pregnant. How could that not be a game changer?

"But I'm eventually going to have a kid and . . . that kid isn't yours. . . ." She waited for him to respond but he just looked at her, confused.

"I'm not sure I get where you're going with that."

"Why would you want to be bothered with a kid that belongs to someone else?" she asked bluntly. Before he could answer, the waiter came to take their order.

"Have you decided?" the waiter asked.

"Give us a few more minutes, please," Adam said, holding up a finger. He turned to Chelsea, looking her square in the face. "You don't think it's possible to love a baby that you didn't create?" The question threw her for a moment.

"Of course I do, but . . ." She let her voice trail off, not sure how to finish her sentence.

"I know firsthand what it's like, considering I was adopted."

"You were?" She'd had no idea. He looked so much like his father with his olive skin and square jaw, it never occurred to her that they weren't related.

"To two fantastic parents who love me as much as anyone could. It doesn't matter who contributes sperm or an egg. What matters is in your heart. The rest is just biology." She'd known for a long time Adam was a great guy, but it took someone special to profess he could love a kid just the same whether it was his or not.

"That waiter is probably going to come back soon," Adam said. "Do you know what you want?"

"The um—um, rigatoni with wild boar ragout," she said, but it sounded more like a question than an answer. She really had no idea what that was, but it sounded interesting.

"I think it's pronounced *ragoo*," he said. She laughed, embarrassed.

"My German's better than my Italian," she joked.

"I'm gonna have to agree with you on that," he chided back. "Wild boar isn't as adventurous as chicken feet, but still." There was a sparkle in his eye as he said it and she knew that he hadn't been stressed at all by their paternity conversation.

Chelsea's pregnancy didn't come up for the rest of the dinner. They talked about Adam's experiences at college, what it must be like to work on a crab boat, and all the crazy things that happen at the Lucky Lady.

"So what's your favorite thing about being in college?" Chelsea asked. Adam thought about it as he twirled the last bite of capellini onto his fork.

"I guess just meeting people from all over. One of

my friends is from a farm in Iowa, another grew up in New York City. My roommate freshman year was from Lebanon. If you've never had Lebanese food, it's freaking bomb." Chelsea chuckled. *He's so lucky*, she thought. *To get the chance to go to college and meet people from every corner of the world.* She was happy for Adam, but also a tad jealous. She'd never even been out of the state.

"What do you miss most from here?" she asked, hoping her little neighborhood had at least one thing worth missing. Adam looked down and smiled into his lap. She watched him curiously until he finally looked up at her.

"You," he said softly, and quickly looked away. Chelsea felt her cheeks tighten as a smile spread across her face.

"Me?"

"Is it weird that I said that?"

"No," she said quickly. "I just . . . I'm just surprised, is all."

"I don't know why, but I think about you a lot. When something cool happens, I wish you were there to see it." Chelsea wondered how many times had she done the exact same thing. More than she could count.

"I was pretty bummed when you left," she said. "I

thought maybe after what happened to Mikey, you'd come back."

"I wanted to, but Gramps was against it and so were my parents. They wanted me to finish school." She nodded. She knew that he would have to go back soon.

"Two more years," he said, as if he could read her thoughts.

"Then what? You don't think you'll stay there?" She couldn't imagine him wanting to come back. There was nothing here for him.

"Chicago's cool and everything but . . . I don't know. I haven't really thought that far ahead." It seemed like a long way off for her, too. By that time, her baby would be over a year old.

"Can I show you the dessert menu?" the waiter asked, interrupting. He handed one to Chelsea before she could respond.

"Thanks," Adam said, and accepted one as well.

"I definitely don't want the gelato," Chelsea said, laughing. Adam chuckled.

"How about we split a tiramisu?" he asked. Chelsea read the description silently, still unsure what it was.

"What's mascarpone cheese?" she asked, unsure if she'd pronounced the name correctly.

"I'm not really sure but it sounds cool."

Chelsea laughed again. "Adventure number three hundred forty-two!"

"We've had that many adventures together already?"

"At least. Starting with the time we found that fishing hook, remember? And we tied it to a rope and stuck it down the storm drain?" Chelsea grinned as the memory came back.

"What were we trying to catch? Sewer fish?"

"Alligators! Remember? There was some movie where alligators lived under the streets and we thought we'd catch one."

"That's right!"

Chelsea giggled as she sipped her water. "That was fun. I can't believe we didn't catch one."

Adam laughed too. "I guess you're right. We probably are somewhere in the three hundreds by now."

The tiramisu was brought out on the center of a white plate with an elegant design in chocolate around the edges. The waiter set two dessert forks down. "Enjoy."

"I don't have a clue what it's gonna taste like," Adam said. "But I like it already."

"Weren't they going to bring one for you, too?"

Chelsea teased as she slid the plate closer to her with one finger. Adam laughed.

"Ha-ha," he quipped, and slid the plate back to the middle. Plunking his fork down in the middle of the slice, he chopped it in half. "There. Just so you don't try anything." She grinned and scooped a bite of tiramisu onto her fork. *Oh my god*, she thought, taking her first bite. *This is one of the best things I've ever tasted.* It ranked right up there with *apfelkuchen*, the rich, moist apple cake she made from her mother's recipe every year at Christmastime.

When they had scraped every last crumb of the dessert from the plate, the waiter brought the bill in a little leather book. Adam plunked down Mikey's credit card, signed the receipt, and walked Chelsea to his car. The door squeaked as he opened it for her.

"Fingers and toes inside?" he asked as she settled into the bucket seats. She wiggled them, showing they weren't in the way of the door. He carefully shut it anyway, just in case.

Watching as he walked around the front to the driver's side, she felt a strangely comfortable feeling like this is where she belonged.

When they arrived at Chelsea's house, she didn't

expect Adam to park the car and walk her to the door, but he did.

"Do you want to come in and watch TV?" she asked, not ready for their time together to end.

"I can't. I promised Gramps I'd help him put together a new bookcase he bought. One of those IKEA things where the directions are just drawings."

"Oh," she said, a little disappointed. "Thank you for dinner. It was really nice being on a real date."

"Maybe we can do it again when I get back. . . ."

"You're leaving?" Chelsea felt a sudden panic that surprised her.

"Just for a few days. My cousin in Ohio is getting married. I'm in the wedding, so I kinda have to go."

"Sounds nice." She pictured him in a tuxedo standing next to other guys in tuxedos. She bet he looked really good.

"Is that a yes?" he asked. "I get to take you out again?"

"That's a yes."

Adam stepped closer to her and planted a sweet, soft kiss on her lips. Chelsea felt her insides tighten. She loved the feeling of his warm breath against her face, his body pressed to hers. The kiss was over too soon and Adam stepped back.

"Good night, Chelsea."

"Good night." Caught up in a surge of emotion, Chelsea unlocked the door and went inside. She gave him a little wave. Without moving the curtain, she watched him through the window as he got into his car, tried twice to start it before the engine took, and chugged off down the street. *Damn*, she thought. Just when she thought life couldn't possibly throw her another curveball, it had.

As Chelsea climbed into bed and pulled the covers over her shoulders, her thoughts turned back to her baby. She'd had no idea that Adam was adopted. No one had ever mentioned it. She could tell he loved his parents and was grateful for all they'd given him. They'd sent him to college and bought him a car and had always bragged about how good he was at Little League and in school. She wondered why his birth mother gave him up. Had she been young and scared and with someone like Jeff who didn't want her to have the baby? Or had she been a good student with big plans to go to college and have an important career, and she figured having a baby would derail those dreams? Keeping the baby is what Chelsea believed was best, but was it? Was she being selfish? If her baby was adopted by people like Adam's parents who could afford to give it every advantage in life, wouldn't it be better off with them than with her?

Thoughts of adoption were still floating around in Chelsea's mind when she woke up the next morning. Luckily her morning sickness hadn't returned, so as she scarfed down a bowl of cereal, she researched more about the process on her phone. There were two types of adoption: open and closed. A closed adoption meant she would have to say good-bye to her child and never see it again. No one would tell the baby who she was. She could have no contact with it unless someday her kid came looking for her.

An open adoption meant she could still see it, visit the family, maybe even join them for holidays and birthdays. She could watch her baby grow up even if she wasn't the one raising it herself. There was so much to think about, so many decisions to make, it made Chelsea's head swim. What if she gave the baby up and regretted it later? What if she kept the baby and it ended up hating the life she gave it? She needed a woman to talk to. She thought about Liz, but she'd seen Liz's reaction when she found out Chelsea was pregnant. She already knew Liz's advice would be to give up the baby. There was Dr. Shollenbrook and the lady at the community center, but they didn't feel like people she could really sit down and talk to. Never more than this moment had Chelsea wished her mother was still alive.

Lauren steadied her foot on the brake of Greg's truck and swung into a parking space on the west side of the prison. It was a monstrosity of a complex, all brick, situated behind a sixteen-foot fence topped with coiled razor wire. Above the gray steel door was a sign that read *Release.*

Today was the day her brother would walk through that door a free man. In a fucked-up system, at least the parole board had gotten it right. Lauren looked down at her phone: 10:23 a.m. Greg had said they would release him sometime between ten thirty and noon. She was early. She was never early. That's how anxious she was to see him.

When the heavy door swung open and Greg exited in the same white shirt and dark blue pants he'd worn the day he was sentenced and taken away in a sheriff's van to serve what they thought would be half a decade,

Lauren blew out a sigh. It was as if she had just exhaled all the hardship and pain her family had survived in the past three years. Now that Greg was out, things would get better. They'd go back to normal. Well, soon anyway. First, they had a score to settle.

"Where's Amber?" Greg asked as he climbed into the cab of the pickup.

"Still at her mom's in Altoona. She wanted to see the baby."

Greg grimaced. "*My* baby," he said tightly.

Lauren could hear the anger in his voice. She could understand why he was upset that Amber would choose to take their kid halfway across the state to see her mother on the day he was getting out. She knew Greg desperately wanted to meet his little girl, Lilah, who was now a year and a half old. Amber had refused to bring Lilah to the prison, so even though she frequently sent pictures, Greg had never seen the child in person. But she could also see Amber's side. When Greg was carted off to prison, it left her all alone to have and raise the baby by herself. All the plans they'd made had been ripped apart. Amber had moved in with Lauren and her mother and lived rent-free in Greg's room. It allowed their mom to spend time with her granddaughter, and

Amber helped out by getting a part-time job as a cashier at a nearby grocery store on the weekends when Lauren could babysit.

About a year ago, Amber's mother inherited some money when a family member died, and bought a little row house in Calvert Hills. She'd begged Amber to leave Greg and relocate with Lilah, but Amber, knowing Lilah would eventually want to spend time with Greg after his release, opted to stay. Lauren surmised that Amber's absence on the day Greg got out was payback for the resentment she felt that he was arrested in the first place. Unlike Lauren and her mother, Amber didn't believe that Greg was innocent.

"Mom's making a big lunch for you. She got a roast and made an apple pie from scratch last night." Greg nodded. She could tell he was only half listening. "Did you want to stop somewhere on the way home?" She expected he'd want to swing by Roy's house for a beer or maybe take a drive over to the Delaware and just sit on the hood of the truck and look out at the calm waters like he used to do, but he didn't.

"I wanna see that guy's place," he said. Lauren wasn't sure who he was talking about.

"Whose place?"

"Her sugar daddy's."

Chelsea was busy making waffle cones for the next influx of customers when the bell over the door chimed and the lady from the thrift store entered. She had an oversize brown leather bag slung over her shoulder that matched her chunky brown wedges. Chelsea smiled, happy to see a friendly face.

"Hi there," Chelsea said as the woman stepped up to the counter.

"Hi. A small basil, please."

"Got you hooked on that one, didn't I?" Chelsea grinned proudly as she grabbed a spoon and cup.

"I crave it now," the lady said, and lifted her dark sunglasses to the top of her head. "Um, by the way . . . I got you something." The woman reached into the designer purse and pulled out something square and weighty wrapped up in a plastic bag. "It's nothing, really," she said as she handed it to Chelsea over the counter. Curious, Chelsea opened the bag and pulled out two books: *5,000 Baby Names and Their Meanings* and *The First Nine Months: A Working Woman's Guide to Pregnancy*. The books were brand-new, glossy, and expensive. Chelsea looked up at her, shocked.

"These are for me?"

"Unless you already have them or something. I just thought you might . . . well, I found them useful."

Useful? Didn't she mention in the thrift store that she didn't have any kids of her own?

"No, no I don't. Wow, um, I don't know what to say. These are terrific. Thank you so much!" Chelsea could feel her heart swelling in her chest. She was usually the one doing sweet things for people, not the other way around.

"You're welcome," the woman said, more relaxed.

"I don't even know your name," Chelsea said, realizing she should by now.

"I'm Sonia," the woman said, and pulled out her wallet to pay for the gelato Chelsea hadn't even started scooping yet.

"No, no," Chelsea said and plopped a big scoop of creamy basil gelato into the cup. "Put your money away. This one's on me." Chelsea scooped a few dollars out of her tip jar to put in the register.

"It just blows my mind how expensive everything is

for kids . . ." Chelsea said as she and Sonia sat at a table by the window. There was no one else in the shop and Chelsea knew Liz wouldn't mind if she sat for a bit and drank a cup of decaf coffee.

"Yep." Sonia nodded. "They say it costs two hundred fifty thousand dollars to raise a child from birth to adulthood."

"Unreal." Chelsea sighed. "My friend Adam got me thinking about adoption."

"Oh?"

"Yeah. He was adopted and his parents gave him a great life. The best. They're even paying for his college. Well, the school gave him some money too because his grades are so good, but they're paying for most of it."

"I thought you wanted to keep the baby. You were going to take parenting classes. . . ." Sonia leaned back in her chair.

"I do. I really do want to keep it. But Jeff—that's the father I'm not with anymore—he said I won't be able to make enough money cuz I only make minimum wage. I didn't believe him at first but I started looking up the prices of stuff. It's going to be hard to give the baby what it needs." Chelsea could see Sonia bristle a little. *There I go again*, she thought. *I'm making Jeff look like an asshole without even trying.*

"I don't think you'll be working here forever," Sonia said. Chelsea appreciated her positivity. She knew so little about this lady and yet she never felt judged by her in any way. Still, that didn't change her reality.

"Where else am I going to work? I didn't even graduate high school."

"You dropped out? Why?" Again, just a question. No judgment.

"My grades were okay and all that but . . . it was hard to get a ride with my dad gone so much and when he was home, we were always out late. Plus, there was this whole other situation with a girl at my school—" Chelsea suddenly froze. Her eyes locked on a figure standing on the other side of the street. Terror gripped her throat. It couldn't be. No, no, no . . . She slowly stood up to get a better look.

"Oh my god," Chelsea murmured, so horrified she could barely manage to form the words.

"What?" Sonia asked, alarmed, as she turned to try to see what Chelsea was staring at.

"I know that guy. . . ." Fear gripped Chelsea and

she could feel her hands start to shake. She quickly set her coffee down on the table and looked back out at the man in the hoodie who stared squarely at them. Greg Foster. He'd come back for her!

"I gotta go." Chelsea turned so quickly, she bumped the table, knocking over her coffee. Sonia grabbed some napkins to wipe up the mess.

"What are you talking about? Who is that?" Sonia asked. But Chelsea was already on her way back to the counter.

"I'm sorry. I can't stay here. . . ." Chelsea's mind raced. What should she do? How could she get away without him knowing? Would he come into the store? "I'm gonna skip out the back and try to catch the bus before it gets dark." Chelsea gasped. She grabbed her purse tucked under the counter and the plastic bag containing Sonia's books.

"Um, why don't you let me drive you?"

Chelsea stopped. Was Sonia seriously offering to give her a ride home? It would be much safer than the bus. What if Greg was waiting for her at the bus stop? Still, she couldn't ask this woman who was practically a stranger to do that.

Chelsea looked back out the window. A city bus idled in the street in front of where he was standing. The hairs on her arm stood on end as she waited for it to pass.

"I live pretty far," Chelsea uttered, hoping Sonia would insist anyway.

"I don't mind. Really." In a cloud of exhaust the bus pulled away. Greg was no longer standing at the curb. Had he gotten on that bus? Where was he? Her eyes darted back and forth, scanning the pedestrians moving along the sidewalk. No sign of him. Maybe getting a ride from Sonia would be a better plan after all.

"You sure? I mean, it's, like, forty minutes," she said.

"It's fine," Sonia assured her.

Chelsea locked the front door and turned the *Open* sign to *Closed*. "Let's go. Fast."

ELEVEN
AN UNNATURAL ALLY

Sonia's Lexus SUV sped down the street, driving through the long afternoon shadows. From the passenger seat, Chelsea watched the side mirror vigilantly, hoping she wouldn't spot Greg following them. She had no idea what his car looked like, or if he even still had one after he got out of prison. Every time she glimpsed a twentysomething guy she thought for a split second that it was him. *What did he want from her?* She wondered. *To scare her? To kill her?* When he was behind bars, she at least felt safe. Now that he was out, nothing would keep him from slipping out of the dark shadows on her walk home from the bus stop or breaking in as she slept. She had no idea how she would be able to sleep at all, alone in that trailer, knowing he could come for her at any time. She wished her father were home. She wondered if she should call Adam in Ohio or even ask Sonia to drop her off at Mikey's store after she packed some things, but would that put them both in danger? Chelsea was pretty sure that Greg wasn't as upset with Mikey as he was with her. After all, she's the one who testified against him. All Mikey could say on the stand was that a guy in a mask robbed and shot him.

"Who was that guy?" Sonia asked.

"Someone I . . . I put in prison. . . . He got paroled early." Chelsea twisted around to look through the back window. She didn't see any sign of him.

"What happened?"

Chelsea wasn't sure how much of the Mikey/Greg/Lauren story she should tell. She didn't want to involve a stranger in her problems.

"Chelsea, I want to help you. I'm pretty sure I can but you have to tell me what's going on. Why was he in prison?"

Chelsea felt strange opening up to Sonia, but she seemed so kind and sincere in her offer to help that

Chelsea found herself explaining the whole thing. How she'd witnessed Greg come out of the convenience store after shooting Mikey, how she'd called the police and testified against him, and how the harassment at school from Lauren and her friends got so bad that she decided to leave for good.

"Mikey warned me Greg was getting out, but I didn't think he'd come looking for me," Chelsea lamented, still scanning the drivers of other cars.

"Sweetie, where's your father?" Sonia demanded to know.

"Working on a crab boat."

"Can you contact him?"

"I tried a couple times to call his cell but I don't think he's getting the messages, because he hasn't called me back. There might not be any service out on the water. That must be it cuz if something bad happened to him, they would tell me. Someone would tell me." She didn't want Sonia to think her dad was a bad father who had just abandoned her and she didn't want to believe that something terrible had happened to him.

"Honey, I think instead of taking you home, I should take you to the police. Tell them what's going on."

The police. Chelsea hadn't thought of that. Would

that just piss off Greg even more? And how could they do anything? Standing on the street staring at a public business wasn't exactly a crime. Besides, it wasn't just her this time. She had to think about the safety of her baby.

"How are they going to help?"

"If this guy is on parole, they're already keeping tabs on him. They can protect you."

Chelsea wasn't sure if that was true. No one had protected Mikey from Greg when he'd robbed the store, and Greg had been arrested a few times before that. But at this point, she had only two choices. Go it alone and hope Greg would give up, or tell the police. At least if she ended up dead or missing, they'd have a suspect.

"Okay," Chelsea said. "Let's go to the cops."

"Can you point out the man you saw?" Detective Miggs leaned forward as she slid a lineup card toward Chelsea. There were six photos of men side by side. Chelsea looked down at the card. All the men looked fairly similar, but there was only one person she recognized. Greg. His mug shot was second from the right.

"Greg Foster." Chelsea tapped Greg's picture. Miggs nodded, her tightly woven black bun bouncing up and down.

"As a condition of his parole, he can't make contact," she explained. "Did it seem like he was going to?"

"We didn't give him the chance," Sonia chimed in. Miggs looked from Sonia back to Chelsea.

"Okay. I'll let his parole officer know. In the meantime, Chelsea, do you have someplace else you can stay? Relatives or friends?" Chelsea sat back, unsure how to answer. She didn't have any relatives and she'd lost touch with most of her friends from school. There was Liz, but she didn't want to tell her about any of this. First the pregnancy, now a parolee after her . . . it would seem like she brought drama everywhere she went.

"She can stay with me," she heard Sonia say. Chelsea looked up, stunned. "I live out in Huntington Heights. We have a security system."

"We?" the detective asked.

"My husband and I, but . . . we're separated, so . . . it's just me." Sonia looked down as she finished the sentence, her voice becoming strained as if she were embarrassed to admit she was on the verge of a divorce.

Chelsea saw Miggs raise an eyebrow as if to run the idea past her. Staying far away in Huntington Heights in a house with a security system was the best possible scenario. Chelsea nodded, relieved. She couldn't believe how nice Sonia was. First the pregnancy books, then the ride, now this? Why would this woman want to get involved in something so messy for someone she barely knew? Are there really people in the world who are just this generous? Regardless of Sonia's reasons, Chelsea was glad that she'd be staying someplace that safe. It wouldn't take much to break into the flimsy, cheap windows at the mobile home. Whatever this woman's place was like, it had to be better than that.

"Good. You see Foster lurking around again, call me. If he does anything that allows me to arrest him on a violation, I will. Here's my card." She handed one to each of them.

"Thank you," Chelsea replied, and tucked the card into her purse. She and Sonia stood up. "I need to get a few things from my house first," she told Sonia. "Is that all right?" She hated to inconvenience Sonia again but she needed a few changes of clothes and her makeup. It seemed a bigger inconvenience to ask Sonia if she could borrow hers once she got to the house.

"Of course," Sonia said. "Let's go now and be done before dark."

In her bedroom, Chelsea stuffed a few items into a bag and then moved into the bathroom to collect her toothbrush and toiletries. When she came out, she saw Sonia sitting on the sofa looking at Chelsea's travel book on Germany. She watched for a moment as Sonia flipped through the tattered pages, careful not to break the already weakened spine. Chelsea appreciated how gingerly Sonia held the book.

Sonia looked up and carefully put the book down. "Ready?"

"Are you sure you want to do this? I mean, you're being really nice and you don't even know me." Her father always said *Never look a gift horse in the mouth*, but Chelsea needed to understand why someone so "together" would care at all about any of her problems. Sonia must be busy with her own life. *How could she have time to drop everything and help me? Who is this woman?*

Sonia stood up and heaved a heavy sigh. She suddenly seemed as uncomfortable as she did the first time

Chelsea met her at the gelato shop.

"I know more about you than you realize," Sonia said, nervously tucking a piece of blond hair behind her ear. Chelsea furrowed her brow, unsure what she was talking about. "I guess I should tell you this now," she continued. "Um, hmm. It wasn't an accident that I came into the gelato shop. I wanted to meet you."

"Why?"

"Because . . ." Sonia paced back and forth a little. "How do I say this? Jeff Clefton is my . . . husband. Soon to be *ex-husband*."

The confession practically knocked the wind out of Chelsea. Had she heard that right? This was Jeff's *wife*? Everything she thought she could trust about Sonia, the appreciation she felt for her help, was suddenly swept away. *What an idiot I am! I should've known not to trust anyone!* Why? Why was this woman pretending so hard to be a friend to her when all she probably wanted to do was to push Chelsea further out of Jeff's life?

"He put you up to this?!" Chelsea was so furious, she could barely get the words out.

"No! Not at all. He doesn't even know I talked to you," Sonia said earnestly. She lifted her hands, trying to calm Chelsea down.

"Why does everyone lie to me?" Chelsea squeaked out, on the verge of tears. She'd wanted so badly to talk to someone that she hadn't questioned why this woman was being so nice to her. "Manipulative" was a better word. Bringing the baby books, seeing her at the store, coming in for gelato . . . this woman had been stalking her! Even the questions about where she got the necklace and if the father liked the name she'd picked for the baby! Chelsea could feel her face flush with anger. All she wanted now was for this woman to get out of her house. She had enough pressure dealing with Greg. She couldn't handle this on top of it.

"Chelsea, I'm sorry. I am! But please . . . just let me explain."

"I want you out! I told you all this stuff about me and—"

"Stop!" Sonia interrupted, more forcefully now. "You need to hear what I have to say!" Chelsea shook her head, still in shock. She didn't want to hear any of it. She didn't care. Sonia could have her worthless husband. He was nothing worth fighting for. Sonia kept talking anyway.

"Jeff doesn't know I'm here. I suspected he was

having an affair and I went to the hotel where you and he met up. I . . . I wanted to see what you looked like. I was shocked by how young you are and I wanted to know more about you. That's all it was."

Chelsea took a step back, remembering her now. She had been the woman in the ball cap reading a magazine in the lobby when she checked in. That first time they chatted at Stella Luna, Chelsea had thought the woman looked vaguely familiar but just assumed she'd been into the shop before.

"Now you know everything there is to know!" Chelsea blurted out. There was so much anger inside her. At Sonia, at Jeff, at herself. She couldn't help but feel embarrassed to be the "other woman." Chelsea felt tears well up in her eyes.

"Please don't cry," Sonia said.

"I said I want you out," Chelsea repeated, and broke into sobs. Big, heavy, exhausting sobs. The kind that take over completely. Chelsea slid down the wall onto the floor and drew her knees into her chest. She buried her face in her hands, blocking as much light as she could. All she wanted right now was to be in total darkness. Instead, she felt Sonia's hand on her arm.

"Go away. Please! Please just go away." Her words were barely intelligible.

"I'm not finished. There's more." Sonia's voice was soft. Chelsea silenced her sobs but refused to look up. "The first day I met you, you were very sweet and I genuinely liked you," Sonia explained calmly. "I went into Stella Luna to confront you, to tell you off for stealing my husband. But as soon as we started to talk, I realized you weren't some evil little home-wrecker like I thought you were. We'd both been played by the same person. I thought I would hate you, but . . . it was just the opposite."

This surprised her. If Chelsea had found out her husband was cheating, she would have hated the woman he was seeing. Then again, Jeff had told Chelsea that Sonia was the one who initially wanted the divorce. Chelsea didn't understand why Sonia would have sought her out when she didn't love Jeff anymore.

"How can you say you were played when you're doing the same thing?" Chelsea demanded to know, hoping to make sense of the situation. Sonia gave her a confused look. "The boyfriend you have in New York," Chelsea continued. "The one you've been hiding from him for months! He knows about him!" This woman had basically tossed Jeff and their marriage to the curb long before Jeff and Chelsea had even met.

"What?" Sonia's eyes darted back and forth, searching Chelsea's.

"You know exactly what I'm talking about! He only cheated on you after you cheated on him!"

"Is that what he said?" Sonia seemed genuinely disgusted. "I don't have a boyfriend in New York or anywhere else. I've been completely faithful our entire marriage." Chelsea could sense from the tone of Sonia's voice that she was telling the truth. "Let me guess, he told you that after you found out he was married." Chelsea nodded. "What a jerk. Jeff lied to you about that. He lied to both of us."

Chelsea finally looked up, a pain shooting through her heart. She could see the anguish in Sonia's features. She knew Jeff was selfish for abandoning her and their baby, but it hadn't occurred to her until now that their entire relationship had been a lie. The vulnerable Jeff she'd met at the bar, wounded by his evil wife and desperately in need of someone to love him, did that person even exist?

"I'm telling you the truth. And I know he's trying to

get out of supporting your baby. That's wrong." Sonia pulled her hand away and leaned back. "You shouldn't let him do that."

"He doesn't want us," Chelsea said, wiping the tears from her face.

"Oh, honey," Sonia whispered, and pulled her into a hug. Chelsea didn't wrap her arms around Sonia, but she didn't push her away, either. She needed someone to lean on right now and anyone would do. She could feel Sonia hold her even tighter.

"So he told you about the baby?" Chelsea asked, still unsure how Sonia could know Jeff didn't want her to keep it.

"No. I learned that from you. But the day after you two met at that hotel, I confronted him. He had said he was going away on a business trip for the weekend but came home early because he wasn't feeling well. When I told him I'd been at the hotel and saw you, he admitted what I'd known all along—that he was having an affair."

Chelsea studied Sonia, ready to hear more. She had so many questions. The anger in her seemed to subside a little.

"And how did you know I'd be at the hotel?"

"I heard him talking on the phone to you, telling you to check in early if you wanted."

"I see," Chelsea said, feeling horrible. All along, she'd assumed Sonia couldn't care less about Jeff. But here was a woman who had been in love with her husband. How gut-wrenching that must have been for Sonia to hear her husband talking to his mistress, planning a clandestine meeting, knowing the man she was supposed to trust above anyone else, was lying to her. Chelsea was starting to understand why Sonia had gone to the lengths she had to find out what she was all about. She had questions too.

"You said your name at the hotel and you were wearing your work shirt, so it wasn't hard for me to find you. I spent hours looking at your social media pages, trying to figure out how the two of you met, what he saw in someone so young . . ."

"Did he tell you how it happened?" Chelsea asked. Sonia shook her head. "Do you want to know?"

Sonia nodded. The least Chelsea could do was give this woman the answers she craved. "We met at a bar about three months ago. He was with his friend Orin. We talked for a little bit and he gave me his number. I guess he assumed I was older than I am." She could see the pain in Sonia's eyes as she spoke. "Do you really want to hear this?" Sonia nodded again, more adamantly.

"He told me that you'd had this boyfriend in New York for a long time and you both wanted a divorce, that it was just a matter of paperwork."

"Of course he did," Sonia exhaled, wringing her thin hands together.

"I'm sorry," Chelsea said. "I didn't know that you would be hurt by me and him . . . doing what we did. I thought you were done with the marriage. I really did."

"I know."

"I'm not trying to take him away from you. I really am done. Even if he is the father."

"I am too. The day I confronted him, I had a divorce lawyer draw up the paperwork." For the first time since Sonia revealed the truth about who she was, Chelsea felt like she and Sonia were on the same side. Sonia was right. Jeff had lied to them both. They had that in common.

"Did he move out?" Chelsea asked, curious as to where Jeff was. She hadn't heard from him since she'd thrown his money all over the yard.

"Actually, no. He moved into our guest room. He

said he needed time to figure out what he wanted to do in terms of getting an apartment, or what."

"But you told the detective you were separated. How can I stay with you when he's living there?"

"He's not. At least not now. Jeff's in the hospital."

"Hospital?" Chelsea asked, suddenly worried. She was angry, but there was a part of her that still cared whether Jeff was sick or hurt. The thought that she could continue to have feelings for him surprised her. "For what?"

"Yesterday he went for a run in the park and was hit by a car. I got the call from a nurse at Bryan Memorial right after I left you at the thrift store."

"Oh my god." Chelsea pictured Jeff lying motionless on the pavement, covered in blood. She hastily pushed the image from her mind.

"He'll be okay," Sonia added reassuringly. "He's in stable condition, a few broken bones, nothing life-threatening. I went to see him this morning before I came in to Stella Luna."

"You did?" Chelsea felt confused again. Were they together or weren't they?

"We talked about you, and us. He wanted me to reconsider the divorce but I said no. I'll hold off until he recovers and gets out of the hospital, but after that, we'll proceed with splitting up our assets and finishing all the legal stuff."

Chelsea couldn't help but admire the finality of Sonia's words. Here was a woman who was not going to put up with a man cheating on her. *She's stronger than I am*, Chelsea thought. *She has her shit together way more than I do.*

"I also told him that he needed to support your child."

"What did he say?" Chelsea sat up a little. She was taken aback that Sonia would make a stand for her baby. There was no benefit to her in doing that.

"He said . . . he needed to follow the advice of his lawyer, and that you had agreed not to name him on the birth certificate."

Chelsea sank back, disappointed. "That's true. I did tell him I wouldn't," Chelsea admitted. "He said he'd lose his job and maybe even go to jail and they wouldn't let him see the baby anyway. I thought if I can keep all that from happening, by not naming him as the dad, maybe he'd see our kid and fall in love with it, and change his mind." Saying it aloud, Chelsea knew it sounded naive.

"Oh, honey, don't do that. He's the father and he needs to take responsibility. If you don't name him, it'll be that much harder for you to hold him financially accountable."

"Are you just saying that because you're mad at him? You want to see him go to jail?" Chelsea wanted to take Sonia's advice but she wasn't sure of Sonia's motives. *She must be as hurt and pissed off at Jeff as I am.*

"No, no. Of course not. I'm saying that because he was as much a part of creating this child as you were. It's not right for him to skip out on taking care of it and stick you with everything. Especially when he can afford to pay for all the things the baby's going to need."

Chelsea searched Sonia's face, still not convinced she should believe her. She was torn between the voice in her head that was asking what if Sonia was just using her to punish Jeff and none of this was for the good of the baby, and her heart, which told her that Sonia was telling her the truth. Chelsea decided to trust her heart.

"Can I still come to stay with you?" Chelsea asked.

A relieved smile broke on Sonia's face and she grabbed Chelsea's hand, squeezing tightly. "Of course you can," she gushed, and hugged Chelsea again.

"Everything is going to be okay. We'll figure it out." Those were the words Chelsea needed to hear. Letting the tears fall, she clung to the woman with everything she had. As the anger and skepticism melted away, Chelsea felt the peace that comes with forgiveness and hope.

Everything felt different for Chelsea as she stared out the car window at the city on her way to Sonia's house. The ramshackle buildings had vanished several miles back, replaced by big, lavish homes nestled behind landscaped lawns. As she watched them pass one by one, Chelsea felt for the first time that the burdens she'd been carrying weren't quite so heavy. And she didn't have to carry them alone. She wondered if it would be weird, though, being in Jeff's house, seeing the table where he ate with his wife, the bed that they slept in. She wondered if Sonia still had wedding photos of them up on the walls and his shoes lying near the door. *It doesn't really matter*, she thought. The feelings for Jeff were fading faster than she anticipated they would, and every time she saw a couple romantically cozied up, walking hand in hand past the gelato shop, her mind drifted to Adam, not Jeff.

Suddenly, the soft music that was playing in Sonia's SUV stopped and an automated voice piped in: "You have a text from Cassandra. Would you like me to read it?" Chelsea grinned. She'd never been in a car that asked if it should read a text.

"Yes," Sonia said in a crisp, clear voice.

"Emergency here. Bulldog hit by a car. Westerly is requesting your assistance." The voice was off-putting and robotic.

"I'll be right there," Sonia said.

"Got it," the voice said, artificially enthusiastic. "I'll be right there." Sonia touched a button, turning off the Bluetooth.

"I'm going to have to go to the clinic first, okay?"

Chelsea, worried for the dog, nodded adamantly. "Yeah, of course," she responded, suddenly remembering that Jeff had told her his wife was a veterinarian. At least he had been honest about *that*.

Within minutes, they were parking in front of the small but upscale brick building with a glass front. Sonia swung the Lexus into a space marked by a sign that read *Reserved for Dr. Clefton*. Chelsea was impressed that she had her own space that no one else could park in, but not nearly as much as she was by calling Sonia "Dr. Clefton." She hadn't known Sonia long, but in the time she had, she'd gone from being the "nice lady who likes basil gelato" to "Sonia" to "Jeff's soon-to-be ex-wife." Now she saw her in an entirely different light—a trained doctor who gets called in to save animals' lives. How cool.

Five minutes later Chelsea found herself standing back in the corner of the sterile exam room, watching as Sonia and a fresh-faced young woman in a lab coat named Cassandra worked to ease the pain of a chubby caramel-colored bulldog. Cassandra pulled supplies from a cabinet, quickly arranging them on a cart as Sonia drew a clear liquid into a syringe from a bottle.

"You're going to be just fine, sweet little Cody. . . . I just need you to relax so I can check for signs of internal bleeding. . . ." Sonia cooed as she squirted the liquid into the IV that was already connected to the dog's paw, wrapped with tape. Chelsea watched, intrigued, as Sonia began to expertly feel around on the dog's belly. As the dog closed his eyes and relaxed into a slumber, Sonia lifted his lip and examined his gums. For a few moments, Chelsea forgot about her own problems, pouring all her attention into Sonia and the dog, hoping Sonia could save its life.

* * *

Less than a half hour later, Sonia was situating Cody in his recovery kennel and asked Chelsea to check on the feral kitten that was sleeping in her office.

"How's he doing?" Chelsea asked, looking up from the tiny, wobbly black kitten she held in her lap as Sonia entered her office with a file in her hand.

"He should wake up in the next fifteen minutes or so. I'll show you the X-ray," she said, and slid the dog's film onto a light box mounted on the clean gray wall. Chelsea stood up, still cradling the kitten to her chest as she looked at the white blotchy area Sonia pointed at. "That rib right there is broken. See? Doesn't seem like there's any internal issues, but Dr. Westerly's going to keep an eye on him." Chelsea nodded, glad that Cody's prognosis was good. She really couldn't tell what was different about the area of the X-ray Sonia showed her, but then again, she couldn't find the baby's feet on the sonogram, either. She guessed that's one of the things doctors are trained to do, see stuff that regular people can't. Sonia turned her attention to the kitten nestled in Chelsea's arms.

"This little furball's name is Hope. A lady found her under her porch and brought her in to us." Sonia rubbed the top of Hope's tiny head with her thumb and the kitten closed its eyes.

"Is she sick?" Chelsea wasn't sure how kittens were supposed to act but this one seemed rather sleepy.

"Nope. But we're keeping her here until she's old enough to adopt out."

"How old is that?" Chelsea asked as Hope settled deeper into her arms and began to purr. She loved the way it felt next to her—so soft and fragile. And she loved that she could make it feel comfortable enough to just fall into a deep slumber. *This kitten is so vulnerable and yet so trusting*, she thought. *It believes everyone who holds it will keep it safe. Hope has no idea what kind of place the world really is.*

"Twelve weeks," Sonia announced, and went to a drawer on the far side of the room. She pulled out a white liquid and began to prepare a bottle for it.

"Is that milk?" Chelsea asked.

"Kitten formula. It's easier on their tummies. Some vets will let kittens go at eight weeks, but I like to wait until twelve."

"So young," Chelsea mused.

"Have you ever had a pet before?" Sonia asked as she handed Chelsea the little bottle. "Put a drop on her lips and let her lick it off, then squeeze just a tiny bit at a time."

"No pets. My dad didn't want one," Chelsea said as she fed Hope. She was careful not to put too much of the formula on Hope's pale-pink little lips, determined to prove she could follow Sonia's instructions.

Sonia stood up and started to pack items into her black leather bag: latex gloves, antibiotic wash, and gauze.

"What's that for?" Chelsea asked.

"It's my vet bag. I keep it in the car in case I come across injured animals as I drive." Sonia filled three empty syringes from a small bottle and capped them.

"That's medicine?"

"Tranquilizer. Some animals, when they're hurt, are in so much pain that they'll bite and struggle if you try to touch or move them. One of the doctors I work with here was bit really badly on the hand by a dog that had been hit by a car. Had to have surgery to repair the damage. Anyway, I only tranq them if I have to. The majority realize you're trying to help." Chelsea couldn't help but wonder if Sonia viewed her as one of the many stray wounded animals she'd saved.

"Maybe we should take her with us tonight. . ."

"Who? Hope?" Chelsea lit up, unable to contain her excitement. "Can we?"

"I'll go get a box," Sonia said and exited, leaving Chelsea alone with the kitten. She looked down at Hope's soft round belly and almost imperceptible little claws that would appear and disappear as she kneaded her tiny paws against Chelsea's hand. There was something wonderful and scary about the responsibility of taking care of this little thing. If someone didn't bottle-feed it and keep it warm and safe, it wouldn't survive. It depended completely on her to make all the right decisions.

At least she had Sonia to tell her what to do. Sonia not only knew how to raise a baby animal to adulthood, but she could bring it back from the brink of death. The way Sonia had come in and taken command of the situation with Cody blew Chelsea away. She'd been so calm, so in control. When they'd first arrived and heard that dog whining in pain, Chelsea could hardly stand it. Her heart rate shot up and all she could think to do was beg the universe to let the poor thing live. But not Sonia. Sonia stayed cool and collected as if it were the most natural thing on earth. *I wish I could be that way*, Chelsea thought as Hope, now starting to doze off, stopped licking the formula from her lips. *I wish I could just always know exactly what to do like she does.*

Once again, Chelsea wondered how she was going to raise a baby, if the thought of taking care of a kitten seemed overwhelming. *Surely she would be able to manage*, she thought. After all, women all over the world did it every day. But Chelsea couldn't quite silence that little voice of doubt that had taken up residence in her head.

Hope slept in the corner of her box, nestled in a little blanket the entire ride from the clinic to Sonia's house. Chelsea glanced down at the kitten a few times to make sure she wasn't being jarred by the occasional bumps in the street, and the rest of the time she spent staring out the window. Finally, after a long silence, she spoke.

"I wasn't at the bar to try to find a guy or anything," Chelsea said. She could tell by Sonia's reaction that the statement seemed like it came out of the blue, but it really hadn't. Chelsea had been trying to think of a way to explain to Sonia why she decided to call the number on Jeff's card even though she knew from the wedding ring on his hand that he was married. She wasn't sure why at this moment she was struggling with guilt again, but she was.

"Okay," Sonia said.

"You know, my dad started bringing me with him to the bars when I was little. He wasn't there the night I met Jeff or anything, though. I don't really like hanging out at the Lucky Lady but, I don't know, it's still better than just being home by myself. Does that make sense?" She looked over, hoping to gauge Sonia's reaction. Sonia just nodded.

"I can understand that."

Chelsea expected Sonia to say more but she let Chelsea continue. "There's a bartender there, Rascal, who has always kinda been like a big brother and watches out for me."

"That must make you feel good," Sonia said casually. "Having someone look out for you like that."

"For sure," Chelsea said, opening up a bit more. "I used to get so scared being home alone. Especially after the thing that happened with Mikey. For a long time I had nightmares that Greg was trying to get into my bedroom to kill me. In the dream, I would try to get my window open so I could get away but it was stuck. I couldn't lift it up at all." Chelsea paused. "Anyway, I just don't want you to think I was out trolling for some rich guy or something."

"I didn't think that, Chelsea."

"When I first met Jeff, I guess I liked him because he was different from most guys. I thought so, at least."

"What do you mean?"

"He had on nice clothes and didn't make any gross sexual comments or anything. He just seemed . . . classy. And nice. But the truth is, I knew he was married. I asked him about it on our first date. Why he wasn't wearing his ring. He had it on the night I met him. But that's the thing. I knew. When I decided to call him, I already knew and that didn't stop me from picking up the phone and dialing his number and I don't know why it didn't." Chelsea waited for Sonia to tell her how inconsiderate and selfish that was, but she didn't.

"Do you think you're responsible for breaking up our marriage?" Sonia asked. That was it. That was the thing Chelsea couldn't bring herself to say. Now that Sonia had said it, the guilt doubled. *I need to say it out loud. I need to be honest and admit that this whole crazy situation started with me deciding to call a married man.*

"If I hadn't called him, I never would've seen him again. So yes. I guess I did."

"How do you know he wouldn't have come back to the bar looking for you?" Sonia asked. Chelsea hadn't thought of that. There was certainly the possibility Jeff could've done that.

"Look, Chelsea," Sonia said slowly. "You didn't break up our marriage. *Jeff did that.* Jeff's the one who took the vow to be faithful to me. Jeff's the one who broke it."

"I'm still sorry. You're a good person. You're letting me stay with you and you save animals and . . . well, you deserve a good guy."

Sonia smiled at her. It put Chelsea at ease. She didn't know how Sonia could not harbor even an ounce of hard feelings for her. But somehow, she was able to see everything that had happened in an objective way and Chelsea was grateful.

"You deserve a good guy too."

When Chelsea heard that, she knew she'd made the right decision in trusting Sonia. She'd never felt this sort of a connection with someone before. Sonia had come into Chelsea's life at a time she felt the most lost. Maybe her mom had pulled some strings from the other side, finding someone who could give her daughter guidance when she couldn't. Maybe the universe just provided it to pregnant teenage girls without them having to ask. Regardless of how it all came about, Chelsea wasn't going to look a gift horse in the mouth.

Chelsea's thoughts were interrupted when Sonia's SUV pulled into a driveway, and she took in her surroundings. *Holy crap*, she thought, staring up at a huge structure with immense windows tucked under pointed eaves. The double front doors sported twin wreaths made of intertwining branches and bright red berries. This is where Jeff was when she would talk to him on their late-night phone calls. This is what he would come home to after their dates, their clandestine meetups in various boutique hotels. It seemed surreal. She'd pictured his house many times, imagined coming home with him after some office party for his work, after they were married. But she'd never pictured it quite like this. This house was much bigger and more stunning than the one she'd created in her mind.

Pulling the kitten from its box, she snuggled it up against her neck and stepped out of Sonia's SUV. Grabbing her worn overnight bag from the back seat, she followed Sonia up the front walk, past the row of small hedges that lined the stone path and to the front door.

The inside was even more impressive than the outside. Chelsea stepped into the foyer and looked up at the glittering chandelier that hung from the ceiling high above their heads.

"You can just leave your bag there by the stairs if you want," Sonia said, picking up the mail from a narrow glass table and sifting through it. "We can take your stuff up later." Cuddling Hope close, Chelsea set her bag down on the marble floor and walked with Sonia through the living room and into the kitchen.

"If you put Hope down, she'll explore the kitchen. Just keep an eye on her so she doesn't go too far."

"Sure." Chelsea gently set the pint-size cat down on all fours. Wobbling a bit, and overcome with excitement, Hope meandered around the room examining every inch.

"If you want to cut up the tomatoes, you can do that, too," Sonia said. Glad to have something to do, Chelsea washed her hands while Sonia pulled out the wooden cutting board. "Knives are right there." Sonia nodded toward a big wooden block sitting on the counter.

Even the knives are expensive, Chelsea thought as she pulled one with a serrated edge from the block. Chelsea turned to take a peek at Hope who was playfully batting at Sonia's purse strap, which looped over the edge of the chair. Satisfied Hope was fine, she began to carefully slice the tomatoes. Chelsea glanced over at Sonia, who looked as much at home making dinner as she did saving Cody's life.

"Can I ask you something?" Chelsea asked after a moment.

"Sure."

"Jeff said you lost a baby. Is that true?" Chelsea tried to say it with sensitivity but she wasn't sure it had come out right. She didn't want to bring up something that was painful for Sonia, but she needed to know if Jeff had lied to her about that, too. Sonia inhaled deeply before answering.

"Yes. That part is. I got pregnant a year and a half ago and I lost it."

"I'm sorry," Chelsea uttered. It was all she could think of to say.

"Thank you. At least he was honest about something, right?" Sonia wore a thin smile, trying to lighten the conversation. "If you asked me what's the one thing I always wanted . . . it was kids." She paused, thinking. "That was a hard time for both of us."

"You would've made a good mom. You remind me a lot of mine," Chelsea responded without even thinking, the words coming straight from her heart. She saw Sonia smile and knew she was touched.

"Yeah?"

"She was a very warm person," Chelsea continued, eager to talk about her mother. "Loved kids. She was always happy. She came here from Germany to be a nanny and met my dad. They fell in love and she stayed. She was only twenty-two when they got married."

"That was pretty brave of her."

"That's what love does, though, right? 'Love conquers all.' That was one of her favorite sayings. Except in German."

"You speak German?" Sonia asked, intrigued.

Chelsea nodded. "I can read it too. My dad speaks it pretty well but when he tries to write it, he misspells a lot of words." Sonia grinned. Chelsea liked that Sonia wanted to know more about her life.

"What happened to your mom?" Sonia asked, and turned on the faucet to rinse off a carrot. A taut feeling crept up in Chelsea's throat.

"She got cancer when I was two and she couldn't have more kids after that. We thought she'd beat it but it came back five years later." Sonia stopped cutting up the vegetables and gave Chelsea her undivided attention. There weren't a lot of people Chelsea could talk to about her mother's death. She rarely mentioned her mother at all to her father because he would quickly withdraw when she brought her up. It was nice to be able to talk so freely with Sonia.

"She always said it didn't matter—that she couldn't have more kids—because I was enough for her. She also said that someday she'd have grandbabies. Only after I went to college and married a great guy, though." The wave of regret that washed over Chelsea took her by surprise. "I guess if she only gets one of the three, it's still okay. . . ."

"That's not really a dream that has to die," Sonia said. "You're still so young. . . ."

Chelsea shrugged. In seven short months, she'd be carrying the baby around in her arms instead of her belly. That was barely enough time to get her GED. And then what? She couldn't take a baby with her to college classes. There wouldn't even be time for college. She'd have to pick up extra hours at Stella Luna just to pay for the baby's diapers and food.

"I read online that teen moms a lot of times don't

graduate and some never get married. They say it makes your life worse, but if you weren't going to have those things anyway, you're not really losing out on anything, right? I mean, maybe in that case, a baby makes your life better." Chelsea put it out there hoping to hear what Sonia had to say about it. If anyone could understand how being a mom could make her important in the grand scheme, she believed it was Sonia.

"You can have those things if you want them. I can help you," Sonia said, and paused. "One of *my* favorite sayings is, 'You can have *anything you want* but you can't have *everything you want*.' You should make your choice based on what you really want, not what you think you can't have." Chelsea hadn't heard the saying before, but she liked it. The idea that nothing was closed off to her if she really wanted it was inspiring. And yet, there would be sacrifices she'd have to make down the road. If she decided to keep her baby, there would be things she'd have to give up, but if being a mother was really what she wanted, she could be successful at it.

After dinner, Chelsea scooped up Hope, who had fallen asleep on the furry white rug that spanned the floor of the living room, and carried her in her box up the stairs. Sonia opened a door at the end of the long hallway and showed Chelsea her room.

Sonia set Chelsea's bag on the bed. Chelsea looked around at the richly appointed furnishings: the queen-size bed with an expensive duvet, oak desk with a matching chair, and double curtains.

"There are three guest rooms," Sonia said. "Jeff was in the one downstairs."

"Oh."

"There are towels in the bathroom and extra blankets in the closet," Sonia said as she fluffed a pillow and turned on the lamp.

"Thanks." Chelsea set Hope's box down. Sonia picked up the kitten and put her on the bed. Hope found the most comfortable spot, right in the center next to a pillow, then curled up and closed her little eyes.

"If you need anything, let me know. I'm going to turn on the security system for the house. If any window or door opens without the code, an alarm will go off and the police are automatically called."

"Okay." Chelsea sighed, reassured.

"I don't think it's a good idea for you to go into work tomorrow. Do you need to call in?"

"I'm off tomorrow anyway."

"Okay. Well, good night," Sonia said.

"Good night." Sonia turned to leave, but Chelsea stopped her at the door. "Sonia?"

"Yes?" Sonia turned back.

"Thank you for everything."

"You're welcome. Get some sleep." With that, Sonia left, gently closing the door behind her. Chelsea sat down on the bed, sinking into the goose-down duvet. Here, she felt safe. Not just because of the security system that would dial the police if breached, and not just because Sonia was sleeping just down the hall and would know what to do if Greg came to find her, but because the burden of life had somehow been lifted from her shoulders, even if only temporarily. Tonight, Chelsea didn't need to worry about anything except taking care of Hope, who snored an almost imperceptible kitten snore. She could take a hot bath and climb into the marshmallow of a bed and just let her mind relax. She pulled one of the parenting flyers she took from the community center out of her bag and began to read through it. She knew she couldn't live here forever. Eventually, she'd have to go back to her father's trailer, to the gelato shop, to being a single expectant teen mother who still had no idea how she was going to take care of a baby. But tonight, wrapped in the warmth of luxurious cotton sheets and protected by Sonia's cutting-edge security system, she felt safe from the world. She had no idea where Greg Foster was, but it didn't matter. He couldn't get her. At least not tonight.

TWELVE

UNJUST REPRISALS

Light was streaming in through the kitchen window when Chelsea entered, fully dressed, with Hope tucked into the crook of her arm. The rich smell of coffee brewing filled the house, though after such a restful sleep, she wasn't sure if she even needed any. Sonia looked up from her tablet and smiled.

"Good morning. Almost noon, actually."

"I can't believe I slept so late," Chelsea said apologetically.

"You must've needed it." Sonia smiled. "Hey there, Hope. . . ." Sonia crossed the spacious kitchen and pulled a white ceramic mug from the cupboard. It matched all the other white ceramic mugs there. "Would you like some?"

"Am I allowed to drink coffee when I'm pregnant?" Chelsea asked as she set Hope down on the floor. Sonia smiled.

"Good question. One cup a day is fine."

"Sure, then. Black, please. Don't you need to go into work this morning?" Chelsea asked.

"Not until three. Dr. Chu has the morning shift today. Maybe you'd like to come with? I've got a spay first up this afternoon and then a teeth cleaning. Thai Ridgeback. Have you ever seen one?"

"That's a type of cat or a dog?"

"Dog. They have big ears that stand straight up and the fur on their back grows in the opposite direction of the rest of their coat." Sonia handed her the coffee.

"Thanks. I've never seen one but they sound cute."

"I'll show you a picture." As Sonia started to search for images of the dog on her tablet, the doorbell rang. She handed the tablet to Chelsea. "Go ahead and look for it. I'll be right back."

Chelsea had just begun to swipe through the photos of dogs when she saw an ad pop up on Sonia's iPad for dog food and remembered she'd left Hope's bottle upstairs. As she padded down the hall, she saw Sonia disarm the security system and open the door. She knelt down and picked up a box.

"What's that?" Chelsea asked as she passed Sonia to head up the stairs.

"It's addressed to Jeff. . . ." Sonia said, intrigued. "But I don't know who it's from. It must be from someone at—"

"Special delivery," Greg interrupted as he stepped out from the hedge where he was hiding and shoved a gun in Sonia's face. In less than a second, he was inside, shoving Sonia up against the wall. Lauren barged in right behind him, gripping a gun as well, and slammed the door shut.

"Oh my god," Sonia gasped, raising her hands in the air. Chelsea froze, shocked.

"There she is!" Lauren said, and pointed her gun up at Chelsea. "Don't move." Chelsea couldn't move if she'd wanted to. Her legs simply wouldn't do it. Greg, keeping his gun trained on Sonia, hurried up the stairs and grabbed Chelsea, pulling her back down into the foyer. Lauren walked briskly toward her until the gun was only a few inches from her cheek.

Greg then seized Sonia by the arm and yanked her to the center of the foyer before pushing her forcefully toward Chelsea and Lauren. Sonia obediently walked toward the girls, hands still raised, her face expressionless. When Sonia reached Chelsea, Greg clutched Sonia's forearm and spun her around to face him so that Chelsea and Sonia stood side by side, looking into the face of evil.

"Now that we're all here, let's get down to business," Greg hissed in a low, gravelly tone. "Here's what happens next. You, Sonia Clefton, are going to write a check for fifty grand to Chelsea. Then Chelsea and I are going to go to the bank and cash that check while my sister keeps you company. Understand?" Chelsea turned her gaze toward Sonia, terrified. *Please don't refuse*, she silently begged Sonia. *He will shoot you. He did it to Mikey and he'll do it to you.* When Sonia didn't immediately agree with his demand, panic began to rise in Chelsea.

"That won't work," Sonia said, her voice steady. *What was she doing? No, no, no!* Greg's eyes narrowed as he stepped in front of Sonia and shoved the barrel of his gun into her cheek.

"Don't fuck with me, lady. I'm not in the mood."

"If you want money, you'll have to do it a different way. The bank isn't going to cash a check that large," Sonia said in a soft, controlled voice. "She'll have to deposit it and wait for the funds to transfer." Chelsea could feel her hands start to tremble, afraid she was about to see Sonia get shot. She was surprised when Greg didn't flip out on her. Instead he just stared into her eyes.

"Then I guess you make that check out to me and I kill you both right now." Chelsea knew he meant it.

"Wait," Sonia said, the steely, calm quality of her voice quickly disappearing. "I can get you your money. We keep cash in a safe-deposit box at the bank."

"How much?" Lauren interrupted. Until then, she'd stayed silent, letting her brother take the lead.

"Twenty-five thousand. But there's also the jewelry I have in my jewelry box upstairs along with my wedding ring; it's well over fifty."

Greg thought for a moment and then whispered something to Lauren. She nodded. Chelsea glanced over at Sonia, but Sonia didn't look back at her. She was observing the exchange between Lauren and Greg. Chelsea hoped Sonia wasn't going to try to outsmart Greg. He was ruthless and greedy and he'd had plenty of time to come up with a contingency plan. She was sure Sonia had no clue what she was up against.

"Okay," Greg finally said to Sonia. "I'll take you to the bank where you'll clear out your safe-deposit box. But Chelsea here is my insurance policy." Chelsea looked over at Lauren, unsure what he meant. "While I'm with you, Lauren takes Chelsea to an undisclosed location. If she doesn't get a text from me by two p.m. saying I have the money, Chelsea dies and so does her baby." Chelsea sucked in her breath, terrified. Sonia didn't flinch. "If you do what you're told, and the money's really in there, everyone's gonna be just fine. Lauren and I will be long gone and you'll never have to deal with us again."

Silence. It was Sonia's turn. He'd basically called her bluff. If the money wasn't there, and Sonia had anticipated alerting authorities at the bank, that plan was now shot to hell.

"Please," Sonia said, the steadiness returning to her voice. "Just wait here. I'll get the money and—"

"Shut up!" Greg seethed, shoving the gun against her temple. "We're doing this my way. Where's the key to the box?"

"In the drawer in the kitchen, last drawer on the

right, in a gray envelope." Greg disappeared for a moment, leaving Lauren to watch over them. Chelsea wondered if Sonia would try to do something now that Lauren was outnumbered. Attack her, maybe? Greg was only a few steps away, though. It'd be risky. Chelsea decided to leave the decision to Sonia.

Only seconds passed before Greg returned with the key. Grabbing Sonia by the arm, he yanked her toward the foyer, almost knocking her off her feet. Lauren, less physical than her brother, waved with her gun for Chelsea to follow. On the way out, Greg snatched up Sonia's purse and car keys. Chelsea glanced back as Lauren yanked the door shut behind them, but not before Chelsea caught a glimpse of little Hope sitting in the kitchen at the end of the hall, watching them, confused.

Chelsea could feel the cold, steel barrel of the gun in her back as Lauren walked closely behind her, steering her toward Greg's truck. Meanwhile Greg was looking around cautiously, as if searching for any signs of spying neighbors, before escorting Sonia to her SUV.

"Stop right there," Lauren ordered before Chelsea could open the passenger door. Chelsea stopped and Lauren grabbed her forearms, pulling them behind her back. A few seconds later, Chelsea could feel something sharp wrap around her wrists. With a snapping sound, they were uncomfortably cinched together. Chelsea figured it was a zip tie and she pulled against it, testing its strength. Whatever it was, it was strong. And impossible to break.

She watched as Greg forced Sonia into her SUV through the passenger side and told her to scoot across and drive. Holding the gun low, just over his lap where it couldn't be seen by a passing car, he got in and pulled the door shut. Lauren shoved Chelsea into the front passenger seat of Greg's truck and clicked the seat belt across her.

"Safety first," Lauren said with a smirk. Chelsea watched as Sonia's Lexus backed out of the driveway and drove off down the street. Lauren started Greg's truck and pulled away from the curb, heading in the opposite direction. Chelsea watched in the side mirror as Sonia's SUV disappeared around the corner and she wondered if it was the last time she'd ever see her.

THIRTEEN
MATTERS OF LIFE AND DEATH

Sonia held the steering wheel in a death grip, her knuckles white as she tried to focus on driving instead of the gun that was pointed at her side.

"Chelsea really won the lottery when she found you, didn't she?" Greg muttered, disdain in his voice. Sonia wasn't exactly sure what Greg wanted. He was obviously interested in money, but she wasn't sure if revenge was a motive as well. Most likely it was, and Sonia was sure that Greg and his sister had no intention of letting her or Chelsea live once this was all over. He had to know Chelsea would go to the police. She'd done it before. Even if they were long gone like he claimed they'd be, it would be much easier for him if she and Chelsea were dead. Still, she needed to try to negotiate. Chances were slim that it would work, but Sonia knew she had to play every card in her hand.

"Whatever you think Chelsea owes you, I'll pay it. Whatever it takes to get everyone back to even," Sonia assured him.

"That's something a rich person would say. No amount of money can make things right. Three years of my life are gone."

"But the next three can be very different. Chelsea's a child. So is your sister. Don't drag them into something that you and I can work out. . . ." If she could appeal to his sense of humanity, perhaps she could remind him that the decisions he'd made today would affect Lauren. She hoped he loved his little sister enough to care. Greg smirked.

"I do like how you think," he said. "Let's start with the bank and see where it goes from there." As much as she wanted to believe him, Sonia was fairly certain he was lying. However, if she could string him along and let him believe she'd give him more, it might buy her some time. The longer she spent with him, the greater the chance he'd make a mistake, and she could get the upper hand or alert someone to what was going on.

Sonia pulled into a parking space near the front entrance of the bank she and Jeff had patronized for the past eight years. They'd started banking there when they moved into their house, and the tellers knew her quite well. Once inside, she could blurt out what was happening anytime she wanted. All she had to do was yell that she was being robbed. They'd believe her and call the police right away. But what if she did that and Greg decided to shoot her right then and there? And if Lauren didn't receive that text by two o'clock, Chelsea's life was over. If she was going to try to take Greg down, she had to make sure that text still went through, and she wasn't sure how she could do that.

And then there were the other people to think about. If she exposed Greg at the bank, there was a chance he would just open fire on anyone and everyone. Backing him into a corner was a bad idea. She didn't want the blood of innocent people on her hands. *I have to let him believe he's in control*, she reminded herself. With no real strategy, Sonia decided to see if the opportunity presented itself inside. Until then, she'd play it cool.

"Just in case you try to pull something," Greg

warned as he typed a quick text on his phone and showed it to Sonia. It was a text to Lauren that read: *Kill Chelsea and run.*

Sonia swallowed hard. Even though he hadn't sent it, even reading the words made her heart pound.

"If that money's not there, or I think you're trying to send some little distress signal, all I have to do is hit send. One button. Clear?" Sonia nodded. "Good," he continued. "Now I'm going to get out of the car. You sit until I open your door. Then you'll get out and walk in front of me." He grabbed the keys. She nodded.

Greg shoved the gun into his jacket pocket, opened the door, and stepped out. She wanted to throw open her door and run across the parking lot screaming for help, but thoughts of that text stopped her. Like he'd said, all he had to do was push a button and Chelsea was dead.

Greg opened her door.

"Move," he ordered. Sonia climbed out and began to walk slowly toward the door, looking around as much as she could without tipping him off, taking in every detail of her surroundings. There were three other cars parked in the lot, one woman standing outside at the ATM, and a man with a cane leaving the branch. She glanced back. Greg held his phone in his left hand, his thumb hovering over the send button. There was nothing she could do yet. Perhaps once they were inside the bank, she could find a way to get away from him long enough to summon help. As they entered the lobby, she saw only one teller working. It was Carla, a short Latina woman with a scar over her eye. Carla had been an employee there for over a year and had never called her by name or had any kind of personal conversation with her. She wasn't sure if she'd be able to convey to Carla that something was terribly wrong.

"Get in line," Greg whispered in her ear as the door swung closed behind them. His breath was warm and smelled like coffee and stale cigarettes. Sonia stepped up into the line behind a man in a paint-splattered shirt and jeans. She could feel Greg pressing his body against her back. Maintaining a smile, she waited for the painter to cash his check, bid a cheery good-bye to Carla, and head toward the door.

"Hi. What can I help you with today?" Carla asked. Sonia stepped forward and leaned over the counter.

"Hi," Sonia responded calmly. "I need access to my safe-deposit box." Sonia looked around. Samantha, the bank manager, was at her desk behind Carla showing an employee something on a computer. Should she make a point of saying hi to Samantha? No. She needed to just act normal. The situation with Greg was too volatile and anything that seemed out of the ordinary might send him into a frenzy.

"No problem. It's Mrs. . . . ?"

"Clefton. Sonia Clefton." Sonia could see Greg out of the corner of her eye. He'd stepped slightly to the side of her and was discreetly glancing around, sizing up the place. As Carla typed something into her computer, Sonia let her gaze drift up, trying to find the security cameras. If she couldn't convey her distress to a teller, maybe she could at least get it on tape.

"I'll ask Brian to meet you at the doors and take you back to the vault."

"Great, thanks." Sonia walked with Greg at her side to a heavy wooden door leading to the back. With a buzz it opened, and Sonia stepped inside where Brian, a fresh-faced teller who looked much younger than his age, was waiting.

"Mrs. Clefton, please follow me." Brian, in a suit slightly too big for his medium-size frame, escorted them back to a vault door. He opened it with a key and they followed him into the large room where gold safe-deposit boxes lined the walls and the only furniture was a single metal table.

Brian walked to the box labeled *3294* and stuffed a key into the upper lock. Sonia retrieved her own key from her pocket and with a steady hand, slid it into the lower lock. They both turned simultaneously, opening the box door, and Brian slid the long box out of its cubby and set it on the table. She could see Greg hanging back, trying to act normal in front of Brian. It worked. Brian didn't suspect a thing.

"Just press the button on the wall when you're finished and I'll come back."

"Thank you," Sonia said, trying to signal him with her eyes. The young man was clueless, though.

As soon as Brian exited, Greg muscled her aside and ravenously opened the box. He seemed to light up when he saw the four stacks of cash rubber-banded together. He grabbed them and shoved them into her purse. "What's the rest of this?" he asked as he picked up her and Jeff's passports and flipped to the photo page.

"Life insurance policies, car titles, our wills . . ." It was terrifying to think that Jeff would most likely soon be cashing in on their assets as the widower whose estranged wife was murdered.

Greg picked up a vintage ring with an opal that belonged to Sonia's great-grandmother. Nestled in an ornate gold setting, the flecks of green and orange inside the stone glittered in the dim tungsten light. Greg tucked it into his pocket and then pulled out a pair of solid gold wedding bands that were once worn by Jeff's grandparents. Greg slipped those into his pocket as well. Then, grappling with the stack of papers, he shoved them into the pocket inside his jacket to go through later. Closing the lid to the now-empty box, Greg stuffed it back into its hole and shut the door. He pushed the button on the wall and smiled at Sonia as they waited for Brian to return.

"Get what you needed?" Brian asked as he entered the room and they both used their keys to lock the cubby door.

"I did," Sonia said, trying once again to give him a sign, a look, anything to let him know something was wrong with this picture.

"Great. Have a good day," Brian said, and escorted them back to the lobby.

"Thank you," Sonia said, turning to him one last time before the door buzzed open and they stepped through. Brian smiled and shut the door.

"Great," Greg whispered. "Let's go."

Chelsea had been riding with Lauren for almost thirty minutes before Lauren decided to speak.

"You're getting what you deserve, you know," Lauren said with a malicious smirk.

Getting what I deserve? Chelsea thought. *I deserve to be kidnapped? To have the woman who's been nothing but nice to me, robbed? How delusional can you be?* Although the comment made her livid, she kept her cool. She had to. Flipping out on Lauren, screaming all the things she wanted to say, would only get her killed. She had to be smart. She had to think like Sonia would.

"You can't really still believe he's innocent," Chelsea said. "Not when he's in the middle of doing it again."

"You have no idea what my brother's been through!"

"Are you gonna tell me what a tough life he's had? Cuz I don't care." It was the truth. She didn't give a rat's ass what Greg had been through. Nothing that had happened to him, no matter how bad, gave him the right to do what he was doing.

"You think you know so much," Lauren spat. "You

don't know shit. Greg saved my life."

So what? If someone saves your life, you're obligated to help them kidnap and rob people? Lauren's out of her mind.

"That's right," Lauren continued. "Our stepdad almost killed me. Greg stopped him and spent two days in the hospital because of it. He finally had to convince our mom to pack up her stuff and sneak out in the middle of the night. When our stepdad stole all our mom's money, Greg's the one who went and got it back. So shut the hell up about my brother! You know nothing!"

Chelsea could hear years of anger and resentment pouring out of Lauren. Chelsea had no idea what that kind of abuse was like. Her father had never hit her. Not even once. She was starting to understand why Lauren would blindly do anything Greg told her to. In her eyes, he was a hero and Chelsea could tell that nothing she said would change that. She needed a new tactic. She had to put the focus on Sonia.

"He's robbing an innocent woman who's done nothing to you. Sonia doesn't deserve any of this."

"That bitch'll be fine." Lauren snorted. "She's loaded. Twenty-five grand is nothing to her, and her insurance will pay for it anyway."

"The insurance isn't going to matter once we're

dead." Lauren couldn't possibly believe that Greg would let them live. How idiotic could she be?

"No one gets hurt if she just follows his directions. If she's smart, she will."

She's brainwashed, Chelsea thought. *Completely brainwashed.*

"How do you think this is going to end?" Chelsea asked, hearing the steeliness in her own voice. She was doing it. She was staying calm and logical the way Sonia could. The meek Chelsea was gone. She had to be strong and take some control. If she could just convince Lauren that Greg would kill them, maybe she'd be so appalled that she'd turn against him. Chelsea's mind raced, trying to find the right thing to say next. "You think we're all gonna hug each other good-bye and go our separate ways?"

"He said everyone would be fine as long as they do what he tells 'em to," Lauren said flatly.

"You're out of your mind. I already turned him in to the cops once. He's going to kill us both unless you stop him!" She waited for Lauren to say something, but Lauren didn't. Chelsea could tell she was taking in everything she said, so she decided to keep going. "And you know what happens if I die? Or if Sonia dies? You are going to spend the rest of your life in prison. If he—"

"Shut up!" Lauren screamed.

"Lauren, if you kill us—"

"I said shut up!" Lauren shoved the gun into Chelsea's face. The car weaved into the oncoming lane until Lauren yanked the wheel back. Chelsea swallowed and turned toward the window, away from the gun. From the corner of her eye, she could see Lauren lower the gun back into her lap and turn her attention to the road.

Nearly an hour had passed since they'd started driving. It felt even longer. Trying to find a sign or marker or anything that might clue her in as to where they were going, she stared out at the sparse landscape. Each car that came toward them ignited a spark of hope in Chelsea, a reminder that there were other people around who might help her. However, as they drove farther and farther away from the city, the fewer and fewer cars there were. If she could just get out of this pickup, maybe she could flag one of them down and they'd take her to the police.

The car slowed abruptly, and Chelsea realized they were turning off the two-lane highway onto a desolate country road that disappeared into a thick coppice of hickory and hemlock trees. Chelsea's anxiety shot up a notch.

"What is this? Where are we going?" she demanded to know.

"You'll find out very soon."

Blinded by the afternoon sun reflecting off her windshield, Sonia felt Greg's grip tighten on her arm as they approached her SUV. He opened the passenger door and waited for her to slide across into the driver's seat. Jumping in, he extracted the gun from his pocket and pointed it at her.

"Drive," he instructed.

"You got what you wanted. Aren't you going to text your sister?" Sonia was certain Greg's story about letting them go was just a ruse to ensure her cooperation, but decided to call his bluff.

"Figured we'd give her the good news in person. Now turn the key and drive."

Sonia's mind reeled as she pulled out of the parking lot and into traffic. She had to think of something quickly; time was ticking away. For all she knew, Chelsea was already dead, her body dumped along some rural road, but she decided to believe that she was still alive. If they were planning to kill them, it would make sense to kill them together. And if that were the case, she'd be better off making a move once she was reunited with Chelsea. They could work together and she'd know Chelsea was safe. If she tried something now, like crashing the car, she risked not finding Chelsea at all. Besides, if she crashed the car she could be injured in the process and he could make it out unscathed. And what if she tried to step on the gas and before the impact, he pulled the trigger, shooting her in the side? Too many variables. *Too many ways that could go wrong*, she thought. It would be better to at least get out of the car.

"Pull in there," Greg said, and motioned to a warehouse they were coming up on. "Did you hear me?" he demanded when she didn't respond.

"Yes." Sonia eased up on the accelerator, letting the car slow down as it neared the turn. She pulled into the parking lot and continued to drive past the monstrous white brick warehouses lined with rolling steel doors and concrete loading docks. There was no one around. Not a soul. *This is not it*, Sonia told herself. *This is not the place where I'm supposed to die.*

"Park there," Greg said, and pointed to a space near the side of a building. Sonia obeyed and pulled over. But before she could shove the SUV into park and jump out, Greg grabbed her by the shirt and thrust the gun to her temple.

"I can read your mind," he chided, and threw open the passenger door. Yanking hard on her shirt, he dragged her over the console and out of the SUV. Greg spun her around and shoved her face against the side of the Lexus. What was he doing? Was he going to rape her first? Shoot her in the head? Forcing her hands behind her back, he snapped a zip tie around them, binding them together.

"What are you doing?" she demanded, trying to form another plan.

"My turn to drive," he said, his voice razor sharp as he yanked opened the back passenger door. Greg shoved Sonia into the back seat and hurried around to the driver's side. The plastic was so tight, Sonia could feel it cutting into her flesh. As the vehicle took off again, merging back onto the road, Sonia had no idea where they were going. All she knew was that her wrists were bound behind her, making it hard to run away, and a crazy man was at the helm.

* * *

Greg's car crunched along the gravel until it came to a stop near a cluster of trees that flanked a small, decaying wood cabin. *We're so far from the main road now,* Chelsea thought. It had been about ten minutes since they turned off the highway. Chelsea had been silently counting the seconds to herself, trying to figure out where they were. A ten-minute drive would be at least a thirty-minute hike on foot back to the spot where she could flag down a passing car. Not impossible, but she'd have to get away from Lauren first.

Chelsea watched as Lauren got out of the truck and came around to open up her door. She pulled Chelsea out of the car by the arm and led her down an overgrown path.

Chelsea looked around, noticing the stillness as Lauren tugged on her shirt, pulling her along. Gnats dipped in and out of the tall grass and Chelsea could feel them land on her arms and neck. With her hands bound, she couldn't swat them away, but they were the least of her worries.

As the path circled around to the left, Chelsea saw a dilapidated wood cabin hidden behind the tall oak trees. The front window was broken, shards of sharp glass jutting away from the splintering frame. Chelsea had no idea what was in that cabin, but she didn't want to find out. She dug her feet into the soft dirt, jerking Lauren backward.

"Come on!" Lauren ordered, wrenching Chelsea's arm. Chelsea grunted in pain. She tried to wrestle her arm away from Lauren, but Lauren shoved the gun into Chelsea's face. "I'll kill you right here, right now. Swear on my life."

The door was unlocked. The bottom edge scraped the concrete floor as Lauren pushed it open. Chelsea stumbled in, shoved from behind by her captor. She was instantly hit by the pungent odor of mold and decaying wood. There was no furniture, just some overturned buckets and crates used as makeshift chairs and a ratty mattress in the corner. There was trash everywhere: fast-food wrappers and cigarette butts and empty booze bottles. It looked like a drug den.

"Sit down."

Chelsea made her way over to one of the overturned yellow paint buckets and sat down. Lauren pulled out her phone to check for a message from Greg. Nothing.

Chelsea could tell she was nervous.

"Can we change this to the front?" Chelsea asked, hunched over a little.

"Change what?"

"My wrists. It's hard to sit like this with my hands behind my back."

"No," Lauren said, annoyed.

Chelsea sat there in silence. Lauren blew out a sigh and began to pace around, kicking at crumpled soda cans. After a few moments, Chelsea decided to try again.

"Please. It really hurts."

Lauren exhaled and studied her. Chelsea looked back down at the floor, trying to appear frail and non-threatening.

"Stand up," Lauren said as she pulled a folding knife from her pocket. Forcefully turning Chelsea around, she cut the zip tie, freeing her hands. Chelsea immediately rubbed her shoulders, which had begun to hurt. Now, back in a normal position, they ached even worse. Lauren pulled another zip tie from her pocket.

"Sit down," she said. Chelsea sat.

As Lauren started to wind the new zip tie around Chelsea's wrists, Chelsea spotted a broken beer bottle lying near her foot. *This is my chance*, she thought. *It may be the only one I get.*

Suddenly, before Lauren could slide the end of the zip tie through, Chelsea yanked her arm away, snatched up the bottle by the neck, and swung it like a bat at Lauren's head. Lauren jumped back, narrowly escaping being sliced open with the jagged edge.

In a fraction of a second, Lauren had Chelsea's wrist in her hand, twisting relentlessly. Chelsea screamed in pain and dropped the bottle, afraid her wrist would break. Lauren may have been smaller, but she was scrappier. And she knew how to fight.

Lauren forced Chelsea's arm behind her back, sending her belly-first into the dirty cabin wall.

"You filthy little whore," Lauren spat, and pulled Chelsea's arm back even harder. "You're gonna pay for that."

Sonia lied curled in a fetal position in the back seat of the SUV, hands still bound behind her back. With her cheek pressed against the cold leather, she could feel every bump as they sped down the highway. Her mind raced to come up with a plan. She could see Greg in the driver's seat, staring intently through the windshield.

He seemed to grip the wheel as if it might try to get away. Physically, there was little she could do without the use of her hands. And slipping free of the binding seemed impossible. It was tight and with every move, it seemed to get tighter. If she couldn't beat him using that method, she'd have to outsmart him. She just needed to come up with a way.

Sonia's gaze fell to her vet bag on the floor. *The tranquilizers*, she remembered. She'd just filled each of those three syringes with enough to put a frightened eighty-pound dog into a deep slumber. That was more than enough to have the same effect on Greg. *How much does he weigh?* she wondered. One seventy? One eighty, maybe? Certainly not more than that. Two injections should do it. If she could just get them out of the bag and into her pocket, she might be in a position to take control.

Sonia rolled over on the seat, taking her time so she wouldn't alert Greg to the fact that she might be concocting a plan. Once she was on her left side, facing the back of the leather seats, she waited a few moments before stretching her arms back as far as she could. Clasping her hands together, she sucked in her breath and bent forward until she could feel the woven handle of the bag.

Sonia ran her finger along the coils of the zipper until she found the small metal slider body and the pull-tab connected to it. *That's it*, she thought. The sound of the zipper opening seemed unconscionably loud. *Please don't let him hear what I'm doing. Don't let him turn around and look.*

When it was halfway open, enough for Sonia to get her hands through, she adjusted her body once again and spread her fingers to search around in the bag. She first felt the gloves, then the gauze. Moving them aside she tried to reach farther but couldn't manage to stretch far enough to touch the bottom. That's where the syringes would be. At the bottom. Sonia grabbed hold of the handle and pulled the bag closer to her. She still couldn't see what she was doing, nor could she keep an eye on Greg from her position. Pushing her hands back just a bit farther, her middle finger finally scraped the bottom of the bag. Sliding it side to side, she stopped abruptly. Lodged against her finger was the round plastic cap of one of the syringes. *Thank god!*

Cautiously disguising what she was doing, Sonia

pinched the syringe into her hand and tucked it up under her thumb. She felt for the other two, found them, and slipped them into her palm as well. Bringing her hands up, she managed to bend her elbows enough to slide the syringes into her back pocket and pull her shirt down over it.

By the time Greg turned off the highway and onto a gravel road, the sun had begun its descent in the western sky. The SUV came to a stop next to Greg's pickup near the cabin. Greg got out. Sonia shrank back as he yanked open the rear door and dragged her out. Pulling the gun from his waistband, he motioned for her to walk toward the cabin. *Is this where they're going to kill us?* Sonia wondered, trying to fight the feelings of terror. *Is Chelsea already dead?*

When the door flew open and Sonia stepped inside, a wave of relief washed over Chelsea. He hadn't killed her. It must've meant that everything at the bank went as planned.

"Sonia!" Chelsea exclaimed. "I'm so sorry."

"Shut up!" Greg ordered, and pushed Sonia down onto a crate next to Chelsea.

"Did you get it?" Lauren asked.

"Twenty-five. Just like she said. Plus a few nice little surprises."

"Good. Let's get the hell out of here." Lauren kicked an empty soda can aside as she walked to the door. When Greg didn't follow, she stopped.

"Get the shovels from the flatbed."

Lauren cocked her head, confused. "What shovels?"

"Do it!"

Lauren pulled the pickup keys from her pocket, but hesitated before exiting. Greg turned to Sonia with a smirk.

"Shovels? What are those for?" he said in a high-pitched, mocking tone. "I guess you're realizing right now that I lied. We're not letting you go." Panic swelled in Chelsea, tears stinging her eyes. As calm as Sonia was, she could see the anxiety in her as well.

"Think about your sister," Sonia said with a note of authority. "How old is she? Seventeen? Is it really worth life in prison?"

"Interesting you bring that up." Greg wandered over to examine a carving in the wall. "That's the very thing I'm trying to prevent. No witnesses, no bodies, no conviction. Thanks to Chelsea here, I learned a lot in prison. Now get up." Greg waved the gun toward the door. Chelsea exchanged a terrified look with Sonia and stood. Sonia went first and Chelsea followed her out. Greg grabbed a heavy flashlight from the counter and brought up the rear.

"That way." Greg swung the flashlight up, casting an eerie pool of light toward a rocky path that led deeper into the woods. Despite the chill in the air, Chelsea could feel the armpits of her shirt damp with sweat. The temperature was starting to drop. It was September and the nights were getting cold. The light was waning quickly and soon it would be too dark to find their way out. Even if they could, by some chance, get away from Greg and Lauren, getting lost in the rambling woods with no coats could mean freezing to death. Chelsea and Sonia were still wearing the short-sleeve shirts and jeans they'd had on in the morning.

Surely someone was looking for them by now, Chelsea thought. At least for Sonia. She'd missed those procedures at her office. *Wouldn't the staff there have called her? Maybe sent someone to her house when she didn't show up?* As she considered those reassuring thoughts, Chelsea realized that even if someone was worried about Sonia they would have no way to figure out where she was. Chelsea tried to push the thought from her mind. She needed to focus on surviving, not on all the ways this could go wrong.

As the three trudged down the path, Lauren caught up with the shovels. She tagged along silently until they came to a clearing where the ground felt soft under Chelsea's feet.

"Okay, stop right here," Greg ordered. Everyone stopped. He pulled a knife from his pocket and held it up, grinning. Chelsea heard herself gasp, unaware she'd done it. Greg chuckled and twisted the knife until the moonlight reflected in the blade. Lauren shifted uneasily.

"Knives are so much quieter than guns," he said, staring directly at Chelsea. "And so much more personal." *He's just doing that to scare us*, Chelsea told herself. *Don't let him win. Don't be scared. You are going to survive this. Your life doesn't end here tonight.*

Greg grabbed Chelsea's arm and spun her around. Chelsea stared out at the shadowy path, flanked by gnarled tree trunks and fallen leaves. With her hands bound behind her, she could feel the slick fabric of his coat against her palms. He pressed himself into her back.

"Don't," Sonia said. But Greg ignored her and brought his mouth down to Chelsea's ear. She could hear the wispy sound of his breath.

"Do you remember the way I looked at you when you were on the stand?" he whispered. She knew instantly the moment he was talking about. She remembered sitting in the witness booth after she'd just been sworn in. She'd glanced over at Adam and Mikey and her dad. Her father had nodded encouragement. Then she'd looked over at Greg, who sat behind the table, dressed in a suit. He'd tilted his head ever so slightly at her, then grinned. It had sent chills down her spine and she had immediately looked away. She remembered that moment as if it had just happened.

"Do you?" he asked with an edge in his voice she hadn't heard before. She nodded. "Know what I was thinking when I looked at you like that? I was thinking about how much I'd enjoy killing you."

Although she was terrified, Chelsea remained stoic. He wanted to terrorize her, to make her last night on earth hell. She wasn't going to let him.

"You're sick," Sonia said. Greg swung around to her and smirked. "You're ruining your sister's life and you don't even care."

Greg's expression turned angry. He pointed the knife in Sonia's face. "I'm saving Lauren's life, so you can't send her to prison like this little bitch did to me." Greg abruptly brought the knife down and sliced through the zip ties on Chelsea's wrists. Then he pushed her aside and cut off Sonia's, too. Chelsea rubbed her wrists, feeling the marks the plastic ties had made. Greg took the shovels from Lauren and handed them each one.

"Greg, what's going on?" Lauren asked. Greg didn't answer. Instead he turned to Sonia.

"Dig. Nice and deep. Right there." Realizing he was having them dig their own graves, Chelsea sucked in her breath and looked at Sonia. To her surprise, Sonia didn't look back. She kept her eyes on Greg and jammed the blade of her shovel into the moss-covered earth. Following Sonia's lead, Chelsea did the same.

"You said we weren't going to kill anyone," Lauren protested, genuinely stunned. Chelsea and Sonia both glanced up at Greg to see his reaction.

"Trust me. It's the only choice we have."

"But Greg . . ."

"Have I ever let you down?" Greg grabbed Lauren's arm. Visibly rattled, she shook her head.

"No."

"Then trust me."

Chelsea could see Lauren shift uncomfortably. *Tell him you won't be part of this!* Chelsea silently begged her former classmate, but Lauren remained quiet.

Greg lowered himself onto a fallen tree trunk and slipped the knife back into his pocket. Lauren took a seat beside him and they watched Chelsea and Sonia dig. Grabbing the handle, Chelsea slid the blade of the shovel into the dirt. As she lifted it up, it was heavy in her hands. She noticed the silence. No din of traffic in the distance, no sounds of animals, just the occasional whisper of cold wind in the trees and the metal blades pounding against the rocky earth.

Chelsea barely noticed the gray mist that drifted in from behind the cabin like long, sinister fingers. Chelsea could feel the palms of her hands starting to blister and her toes going numb. The cold wetness had soaked through her flimsy tennis shoes. She glanced over at Sonia, who looked back and gave her a slight nod. What was she trying to tell her? Chelsea didn't understand. Chelsea furrowed her brow, trying to convey her confusion to Sonia, but Sonia just looked down at her shovel. Suddenly, Sonia let out a pained gasp and dropped to her knees.

"Sonia?" Chelsea screamed. She knelt down. Greg jumped up and pulled his gun.

"Follow my lead," Sonia whispered to Chelsea. She barely got the words out by the time Greg approached, the gun pointed stiffly at them.

"Get up now!" Greg slid his finger onto the trigger.

"I can't," Sonia muttered, breathless. "I can't do any more of this."

"Get your ass up and keep digging!"

Chelsea stole a glance at Lauren, who was standing a few yards away, watching the exchange. She seemed frightened, a completely different Lauren than the one who had thwarted her attack in the cabin. It came to Chelsea in a flash, and she knew exactly what to do. Tightening her grip on the shovel, she raised it up and swung it at Greg, smashing him violently in the arm. The force sent him into Sonia, who grabbed his shirt and pulled him down to the ground.

Lauren jumped back, shocked. She pointed her gun into the air and fired. The shot echoed through the dark woods, making it sound as if it were coming from all directions. It made no difference. Chelsea wasn't even sure if Sonia heard it.

Wrestling on the ground with Greg, Sonia scrambled to get control of Greg's gun. Chelsea gripped his arm, trying to pry him off, when she suddenly felt Greg go limp.

Sonia pulled an empty syringe from his side. Then she shoved her hand into her pocket and pulled out another one. Greg eyed her groggily and tried to sit up. Sonia bit off the cap and spit it into the weeds before plunging the needle into Greg's neck. Chelsea recognized the syringes from the day before.

"Greg?!" Lauren cried, clearly terrified they'd killed him.

He collapsed against Chelsea's legs, his eyes rolling back. His fingers unfurled and his grip relaxed. Sonia pushed Greg off and snatched up the gun.

Lauren lumbered back a few steps in utter panic. She pointed the gun at Chelsea, her hand shaking wildly.

"Chelsea!" Sonia yelled. Chelsea felt Sonia grip her arm, pulling her toward the trees. Night had started to close in and it was difficult to see where they were going. Chelsea's feet slammed against the ground right behind Sonia's. Running as fast as she could through the murky fog, Chelsea could hear the hammering of

Sonia's breath. Ducking under low limbs and straining to see the path ahead, their feet pounded over the ground until Chelsea stumbled, her toe catching on a rock. Pitching forward, she hit the ground hard and let out a pained cry.

"Chelsea!" Sonia turned around and raced back. "Are you okay?"

Chelsea lifted her hands, blistered and muddy, and grabbed Sonia's hand. She felt Sonia heave her to her feet and a warm trickle of blood against her leg.

"I think so," Chelsea said, and the two continued to run deeper into the forest. Sonia peered back once and kept going. Chelsea, unsure if Lauren was coming after them, didn't bother to look. All she could think about was getting away.

As they reached a small clearing, Sonia stopped running and doubled over, trying to catch her breath. Chelsea stopped too. Her legs were heavy and she could barely get enough air into her lungs. The front of her pants were wet and sticky from her bloody knees. She'd never been especially fit, but she'd always been able to run farther than this. The pregnancy was affecting her.

Where were they? The fog was worse here and she could barely see anything through the dense haze.

Chelsea shivered. She was wet and cold and tired. The sudden howl of a coyote caused her to jump. Where was it? It sounded so close. And threatening.

"Sonia?" Chelsea whispered, scared to move.

"It's okay," Sonia said. "Just a coyote. It won't attack unless you corner it." Chelsea held her breath and listened intently. She thought she heard the snapping of twigs in the distance. Sonia must've heard it too because she pulled Chelsea behind a gnarled bush and knelt down. Hidden away, they could finally talk.

"Stay still. I think that was her," Sonia whispered, peeking between tangled limbs, searching for Lauren.

"Is Greg dead?" Chelsea asked, careful to keep her head down. She shivered again.

"No," Sonia said, and rubbed Chelsea's bare arms to create friction. "That was the sedative from my vet bag. He won't be knocked out for long." Chelsea swallowed, hoping he wasn't already up and searching for them.

"What do we do? Keep going?"

"Just stay here," Sonia whispered, and positioned the gun in front of her, ready to shoot if she saw Lauren emerge from the blackness. Chelsea had forgotten that Sonia had picked up Greg's gun. For a moment, she felt relieved.

Unable to see, they stayed silent, listening. It was getting dark quickly now. The last of the cool-blue light had drained from the inky sky. Every gust of wind that sent dead leaves scattering over the ground made the hair on Chelsea's neck stand on end. Had Lauren stayed to help Greg? Or had she chased after them, ready to finish what her brother had started?

"Lauren?!" Greg's voice was distant but it rang through the night like a gunshot. Chelsea shrank back. He was awake and he was looking for his sister. That had to mean she had followed them into the grove.

Sonia moved slightly, trying to get a better view. Then suddenly Sonia raised the gun and pulled back the hammer. They could see someone standing at the edge of the clearing, silhouetted in the pale moonlight. Chelsea held her breath. Her heartbeat picked up.

Sonia trained the gun on Lauren, who had no idea she'd just become a target. She walked slowly into the clearing, looking around, gun poised and ready to shoot. Chelsea closed her eyes. *Please don't let her find us. Please.*

Lauren suddenly stopped moving. Chelsea tucked back, worried she'd sensed their presence. Every passing second felt like an eternity as Lauren quietly, unknowingly came closer. Her heavy boots crunched over the fallen twigs and dried leaves. Chelsea glanced at Sonia, who never took her eyes off Lauren. Would Sonia really shoot and kill someone? Could she?

At about ten feet away, Lauren stopped again. She lifted her gun higher and scanned the trees. Chelsea held her breath. She could tell Sonia was holding hers, too. Then, as if she heard them breathing, Lauren looked right at them. A shot rang out and the tree bark exploded only inches from Sonia's head.

Sonia and Chelsea instinctively dropped. A second shot cut through the night! This time it hadn't come from Lauren. The gun in Sonia's hand jolted up and Chelsea could smell the burst of gunpowder. Lauren staggered back.

"Greg!" Lauren yelled for her brother as she fell onto her knees and then forward onto the ground. Chelsea could see the girl moving, struggling to turn and crawl back out of the woods the way she'd come.

Sonia leaped up and ran over to her. She kicked the gun from Lauren's reach and knelt down beside her.

"Help me," Lauren begged. Chelsea abandoned the hiding spot and met Sonia at Lauren's side. She looked down into Lauren's eyes and saw the fear of a young woman who believed she was about to die. The same fear, Chelsea thought, that Lauren must've seen in her eyes a few hours earlier. Why should Sonia help the girl who tried to kill them? They should walk away and let her die. But there was another part of Chelsea that couldn't help but feel compassion. Lauren had believed her brother's lies the same way Chelsea had believed Jeff's.

"Do you have a phone?" Sonia asked Lauren as she opened her jacket and examined the hole in her side.

"My pocket," Lauren said. "Where's my brother?" Ignoring the last question, Sonia extracted Lauren's phone and handed it to Chelsea.

"Stay still for me. I need to put pressure on your wound to slow the bleeding."

Chelsea's fingers were so cold she could barely feel the screen. She typed 911 into Lauren's keypad, but nothing happened.

"No service," Chelsea reported to Sonia.

"Keep moving around till you find some. Hurry." Chelsea saw Sonia turn her attention back to Lauren, who kept bringing her head up from the muddy grass to try to see her wound. Even in the dark, she could see that Lauren was losing a lot of blood. Chelsea began to run. Another cold wind whipped through the pines and seemed to cut through her like a knife. As Chelsea dialed the paramedics again, she looked back just in time to see a figure lumbering through the fog.

"Sonia!" Chelsea screamed, her voice getting lost in a gust of wind. Greg grabbed Sonia by the collar, knocking her away from Lauren. He gripped Sonia's throat. Chelsea ran toward them.

"You bitch!" he yelled as he banged Sonia's head against the ground.

"Stop!" Chelsea screamed, horrified. She searched the dark ground for Sonia's gun. She saw the silver barrel glimmering a few feet away. Snatching it up, she aimed at Greg and without thinking twice, pulled the trigger. A bright orange flash erupted from the muzzle. It all happened so fast, and yet it felt like it was happening in slow motion.

Greg sat up and stared right at Chelsea. Blood began to soak through his coat and he looked down at his sister.

"Greg!" Lauren cried, reaching out to him.

Chelsea's hands shook, her grip on the gun so tight, it hurt. Her feet wouldn't allow her to move. Greg looked back at Chelsea and then slumped to the side.

Sonia rolled Greg off her. She got on all fours and coughed as she tried to fill her lungs with air. Lauren, sobbing, let her head fall back into the grass and stared up at the sky. Greg was still. So still. The fabric of his jacket rustled in the cold night air.

It felt like Chelsea was up in the atmosphere somewhere looking down on the horrific scene, completely disconnected. For a few moments, she couldn't feel anything. Then it all came rushing back and she was there, at the center of it all. *She'd just killed Greg. She'd just shot and killed a person.* She felt the icy blasts of wind blowing through her hair, the metal grip of the gun in her palm, the heavy, wet, bloody jeans that clung to her thin legs. Trudging over the muddy ground, she ran over to Sonia.

"Are you okay?" she asked, breathless.

Sonia nodded, still holding her throat. Chelsea looked over at Greg. His lifeless eyes stared up into an expansive sky full of stars. Slowly, deliberately, she raised the phone and dialed again. This time, she heard a ring and finally a voice.

"Nine-one-one, please state your emergency."

"I need ambulances and the police," Chelsea explained. "One man's dead, and two people are hurt. I don't know where we are. It's a wooded area and we're pretty far off a main road." The dispatcher said to stay on the line and she'd triangulate the call. Sonia went back to putting pressure on Lauren's wound and Chelsea dropped down into the grass next to her, answering the questions the dispatcher asked.

"We're going to get you help, okay?" Sonia said to Lauren, trying to keep her calm. "They're sending an ambulance for you."

Chelsea waited for Lauren to ask if Greg was dead, but she didn't. *She must already know*, she thought. As Chelsea watched Sonia do everything she could to save Lauren, she found herself sliding her hand over her belly, her thoughts drifting to her unborn baby.

She'd just ended someone's life, saved another, and felt the vibrancy of a third that had no idea yet how violent this world could be. And also how kind. As she studied Sonia, still working to save the girl who'd almost killed them both, the same woman who had taken her husband's mistress into her home, Chelsea was overwhelmed with emotion. The level of cruelty that Greg could exact on a total stranger was staggering, but so was the level of generosity and selflessness that Sonia possessed. Such extremes. *Life is all about choices*, Chelsea thought.

Chelsea sat there in the wet grass, her hands resting gently on her stomach until she heard the sound of a helicopter in the distance. Moments later, she saw the spotlight illuminate the tree line against the inky sky. As the helicopter circled around, she could hear sirens, faint at first, and then louder. Finally, she saw flashlights shimmering through the trees like giant fireflies as a wave of EMTs and police officers raced toward them.

FOURTEEN
THE BIRTH

Chelsea was careful not to disturb the IV in her hand as she repositioned herself onto her side. Maneuvering in the hospital bed with all her tubes and monitors connected was a challenge, but she wanted to watch as Sonia sat in the nearby chair and held her newborn baby girl.

"She's beautiful, Chelsea." Sonia smiled lovingly at the dainty little infant in her arms, wrapped snugly in a blanket. Chelsea smiled. Although the labor process had gone on longer than she'd expected, Sonia had been there with her every step of the way. A few days before she was due, Chelsea and Sonia had decided to call Jeff and let him know his child was about to be born and she'd found out the gender—it was a girl. When he didn't answer, Chelsea left a message. Jeff never returned her call.

Feeling emotional, Chelsea had been sitting at home watching television with Adam when she'd suddenly burst into tears thinking about it.

"Do you think he'll just show up?" Chelsea said as Adam put his arm around her and pulled her closer. "Would he really miss the birth of his only child?" No matter how she tried to look at it, she couldn't wrap her head around the idea that someone could know their daughter is being born and not want to be there when it happened.

"The people who care about you and care about this kid are going to be there. Those are the ones who will be important in this baby's life, for her whole life."

Chelsea nodded, knowing Adam was right. He was such an amazing guy with an incredibly grounded view of the world. He could always see the bigger picture, and never lost his positivity. Over the past months, they'd grown even closer. A few days before she'd given birth, she had gone over to his grandfather's house to have a pot roast for dinner with Mikey. They were watching old reruns of *Three's Company*, Mikey's favorite show from the seventies, when Adam leaned close and laced his fingers in hers.

"I love you," he whispered into her ear. A warm feeling came over Chelsea's entire body. Everything about hearing those words from Adam felt so natural.

"I love you too," she said, and kissed him softly on the lips. She felt his hand move to her belly and knew that he loved the baby as well.

"She has your eyes," Sonia said, studying the baby. "And, of course, your hair." She laughed. That was undeniable. Chelsea's baby had come out with a tiny shock of straight red hair, just like Chelsea's.

Chelsea watched Sonia with the baby, and even though a tiny little part of her heart ached, she knew she was doing the right thing. She had no idea until she'd seen her child for the first time that it was possible to feel so much love. It was as if every cell in her body was about to burst with emotion for this itty-bitty human being. And it was because of that feeling that she was able to make the decision she'd made.

"I'd like you to adopt her," Chelsea said, hoping Sonia would say yes. They discussed it before, in more general terms, and Chelsea knew Sonia was thinking of adopting. She also knew from the many conversations she'd had with her and from the way she'd taken Chelsea under her wing and become a surrogate mother to her, that Sonia would give this baby a home and a life that Chelsea simply couldn't. Sonia looked up at her with amazement. Chelsea smiled.

"You're going to be a wonderful mother, Chelsea. I wouldn't tell you that if I didn't think it was true," Sonia said.

"I know I would," Chelsea responded. "And that's why I want you to raise her. It's the best gift I could possibly give this child. You are the most selfless person I've ever met. And I trust you completely. Besides, I know you'll let me be a part of the baby's life." Chelsea saw Sonia's eyes glisten as she looked back down at the baby. "You're the only one I'd give this child to. It's the right decision. I know it is. Do you want to be her mother?"

"Oh god," Sonia said as the tears broke loose and

rolled down her cheeks. “More than anything.” Chelsea felt the tears come too as she watched Sonia look down at the baby with new eyes—the eyes of a mother. For a few minutes, the two just cried.

“What are you going to name her?” Chelsea asked.

“I want you to name her,” Sonia said.

“Annette. After your grandmother.” Sonia gasped and reached out her hand to squeeze Chelsea’s.

“I will give this baby everything,” Sonia assured her, dabbing at her eyes with a tissue. “You can see her anytime you want.” Chelsea nodded, knowing Sonia meant that.

The door opened and Chelsea’s father entered with a bouquet of flowers. Adam was right behind them with a big bouquet of pink balloons.

“Dad!” Chelsea said, happy to see him. He’d arrived that morning from a job in New Orleans. Adam had picked him up from the Amtrak station.

“Did you ask her?” Adam inquired, noticing that both Chelsea and Sonia were in tears.

“She said yes,” Chelsea said, nodding.

“This is the best day of my life,” Sonia said in almost a whisper.

"Congratulations," Adam said. Chelsea's father smiled too and then hugged his daughter.

"I'm proud of you, honey," he said, then turned his attention to Sonia. "I know you'll take real good care of my granddaughter."

"You can count on it," Sonia said, and stood up with the baby. "I'll let you guys talk."

"I'll go with you," Adam said. Sonia delicately placed the baby in Adam's arms and they exited, leaving Chelsea alone with her father.

"I'm glad you're here," Chelsea said as her father took a seat next to her bed.

"Me too." He looked around the room. "The last time I was in a room like this, your mother was giving birth to you."

"I wish she could have seen the baby."

Chelsea watched as her father teared up for a moment, letting the bottled-up pain of losing his wife bubble to the surface. She placed her hand on his and let him cry. When he finally regained his composure he looked up at Chelsea.

"Your mother was an incredible woman. Nobody will ever compare. But you're turning into a pretty incredible young lady yourself. How'd I do it? All by myself? I don't know."

Chelsea's heart went out to her dad.

"You taught me how to love, Dad. *Liebe überwindet alles.*"

"It sure does."

FIFTEEN
LOVE CONQUERS ALL

A soft summer breeze lifted little Annie's fine wisps of red hair as she sat on the blanket Sonia had spread out on the lush grass. Sonia looked so relaxed as she smoothed the wrinkles out of the one-year-old's sundress and adjusted her little hat.

"Have you talked to Jeff at all?" Chelsea asked, sipping the lemonade Sonia had packed in the picnic basket.

"Nope. Orin said he was fired for showing up to work drunk and he was spending almost every weekend in Atlantic City. I don't know. I don't get it." In the year since Annette was born, Jeff had appeared and then disappeared from Chelsea's and Sonia's lives a few times. He'd shown up for the divorce proceedings and called Chelsea once but hung up after she answered. He seemed lost, confused, searching for something that even he couldn't define.

"Wow," Chelsea said, dismayed. He was so much different from the man she'd met at the bar two years earlier.

"Let's just say you've traded up." Sonia smiled and nodded behind Chelsea. Chelsea turned to see Adam parking his car on the street.

"That's true. I did," Chelsea mused. Every time she saw Adam, she could feel herself light up. After the baby was born and Chelsea had returned to her father's trailer, Adam went back to school to finish his degree. He'd encouraged Chelsea to get her GED, and she had. Every night, they'd video chat online; sometimes Adam would help her with her homework and sometimes they would just visit about nothing.

But that was all about to change. Adam graduated college and was in the process of moving back. He'd been staying at Mikey's until he could find them an apartment. And then they were going to move in together and eventually get married. But that was after one very big event: Düsseldorf. Adam had surprised her with plane tickets when she'd come to see him graduate from the university. They were going for two full weeks, and she'd finally be able to see the town where her mother grew up. As Adam approached, Sonia gave Chelsea a hug.

"Have a great time in Germany," Sonia said, beaming with excitement.

"Thank you so much. I can't believe I'm actually going."

"I can."

Adam sat down next to them and tickled Annie, making her laugh.

"Ready? We should head out. Looks like traffic's bad around the airport," he said. Chelsea nodded and gave Annie a hug.

"Bye, Annie. Be good for your mama."

"See you in a couple of weeks." Sonia smiled.

As Adam took Chelsea's hand and walked with her to the car, Chelsea looked back at Annette. Sonia took the little girl's chubby hand and made her wave good-bye. Chelsea smiled and blinked back tears. In only nineteen years, so much had happened. She had survived and endured and finally, she felt like she was starting to become the woman she always wanted to be.

The ordeal with Greg Foster was over. Lauren had received five years in prison for her part in the kidnapping. At the trial both Sonia and Chelsea testified on her behalf. They knew that she had been under her brother's thumb and wasn't fully aware of his plan. On top of that, she'd lost her brother—though she would have lost him anyway, since if he hadn't died that night in the woods, he would've been sentenced to life for double kidnapping and attempted murder.

The man Chelsea thought she'd loved and who fathered her baby was out of her life for good. She wished him well but was glad that she wasn't married to him like she'd originally wanted. It would have been a difficult life for her and the baby even without Jeff's recent issues with gambling and drinking. Instead, she was in love with someone solid, someone she'd admired for years. The playmate she had as a child was now her best friend and boyfriend. She was sure her mother would've been proud of that.

Her father was still the same father she'd always had. He still rushed off to various jobs around the country and spent his nights chasing women at the Lucky Lady.

That was never going to change. But in the hospital room, after she'd given birth to Annette, he'd had a breakthrough that Chelsea knew he'd needed to have for a long time. He allowed himself to remember her mom, to relive the beautiful memories that had become painful after her death. Even if her father never found love again, he was more whole now than he'd been in a long time.

And then there was Annette. Chelsea had wondered if she'd ever regret her decision to give the baby up. But that moment hadn't come. Every time she saw little Annie with Sonia, she was reminded that she'd chosen the most loving, doting mother she could and that her child was truly happy. Maybe someday she and Sonia would decide to tell Annie the truth, that Chelsea was really her biological mother instead of "Auntie Chelsea," as Sonia affectionately referred to her. But that would be when Annette was much older and the time was right. For now, her baby was happy and healthy, the future with Adam was bright, and the world was finally in balance.